MADNESS IN MUMBAI

Madness in Mumbai (Rupa Publications) is **Vrushali Samant**'s fourth novel. Her previous book *Prime Time Crime* (Vishwakarma Publications) has been optioned for a book-to-screen adaptation, while *He Loves Me Not* (Penguin Random House, India) was featured at the MAMI Mumbai Film Festival's Word-to-Screen Market. Vrushali's debut novel, *Can't Die for Size Zero* (Rupa Publications), was a runaway bestseller, and she was invited to write a column for *Marie Claire India* titled 'Big Girl in a Skinny World'. This year-long global initiative featured contributors from New York, London, São Paulo, and Melbourne, with Vrushali from Mumbai writing its India chapter. She has also contributed to *Harper's Bazaar*'s special issue on body positivity.

Vrushali won Best Director at the Berlin Indie Film Festival for her debut short film, *Bena* (2022), which was showcased on Disney Hotstar and JioCinema. Her film credits include research for the Hindi feature film *Daddy* (2017), a gangster biopic directed by Ashim Ahluwalia. She has co-written the indie feature film *My Birthday Song* (2018) with actor and director Samir Soni. Her screenwriting journey began on Vikram Bhatt's film *Shaapit* (2010) as an associate.

She started her professional career as an entertainment reporter with CNBC TV-18 and then moved to NDTV. She has written and produced non-fiction for MTV.

Currently a student of screenwriter, actor and director Boman Irani's online screenwriting class Spiralbound, Vrushali has had the privilege of attending guest lectures by Indo-Canadian novelist and playwright Anosh Irani through the programme. She considers it an honour to be guided by these two esteemed figures as she navigates her writing journey.

MADNESS IN MUMBAI

When Forty Gets Naughty

Vrushali Samant

RUPA

Published by
Rupa Publications India Pvt. Ltd 2025
7/16, Ansari Road, Daryaganj
New Delhi 110002

Sales centres:
Bengaluru Chennai
Hyderabad Jaipur Kathmandu
Kolkata Mumbai Prayagraj

P-ISBN: 978-93-7003-799-1
E-ISBN: 978-93-7003-351-1

First impression 2025

10 9 8 7 6 5 4 3 2 1

The moral right of the author has been asserted.

Printed in India

For
Aai-Baba

Mid-way upon the journey of our life,
I found myself within a forest dark
For the straightforward path had been lost

Dante Alighieri
The Divine Comedy

Prologue

The digital camera on the broad headboard of the bed inched ahead with every thrust. And now it was close to the edge. Despite the ecstasy of intercourse, she was aware of the risk of it crashing to the floor. So, she stretched her arm and shoved the camera towards the wall. Another thrust. And the camera started to inch its way back. However, by now she knew there was plenty of time for it to come towards the edge.

There was no reason for her to be in his room. But the chemistry between the two was so torrid that neither of them could resist. There was no conversation from the moment they had met—just voracious hunger for each other.

In the throes of rampant esctasy now, he did not care if his people heard the sounds they made. Consumed by unbridled passion, she had never felt this lustful before. He gave it to her. Hard, raw and untamed. She, on the other hand, voiced risqué compliments about his prowess and well-endowed genitalia in chaste honey-toned English. And that excited him even further.

Moments later, they escalated into an earth-shattering orgasm, and that was when the guttural grunting stopped. In the brightest hour of noon, exhausted by lust, their bodies involuntarily bundled up in bed.

After regaining their bearings, he pecked her forehead and asked what she'd like to eat. Reaching out for the camera she said, 'Nalli nihari and boti kebab.'

~

'Are you out of your mind, Monica?!' her friend Tara, the not-so-famous tarot-card reader, exclaimed, and Monica froze that moment in her camera frame.

'Stop it and get serious!' Tara fumed as she put her chopsticks down on the plate. Monica had just told Tara about her forbidden carnal bash, the following day.

They were at the exquisite Wasabi by Morimoto at Mumbai's heritage five-star hotel, the Taj. It being a weekday afternoon, the tables were buzzing with lunching ladies from the champagne set of the island city. Prim and trim, they ate less and talked more as they flashed their rock-sized sparkling diamonds and exclusive collection of accessories—bags, shoes, watches and sunglasses that were still perched on their heads. However, Monica was one of those beauties who did not need make-up or brands to announce her wealth. Dusky, with a chiselled nose, high cheekbones and a thick mop of long jet-black hair offset with a fringe—her patrician features and dignified aura gave away her old money heritage.

Tara gently slapped Monica's hand. 'Monica, you are playing with fire.'

An impish grin flashed across her chocolate-brown face as she kept her camera in its case. She bit her lower lip and picked up her chopsticks. There was a distinct glow about her.

After all, no amount of cream or make-up can recreate the natural radiance that comes from post-coital bliss. And the more forbidden the copulation, the greater the inner glow.

Breaking her trance, Tara moved in closer and hissed, 'Damn it, he is a gangster!'

'But the sex is so good. It is the best I have ever had.' Saying this, Monica took a sip of her jasmine tea.

Tara opened her mouth to say something. However, she was unable to find words. She noticed a certain new-found composure in her...er...well...friend. Of course, there was a vast difference in their financial status. And age as well. In her late twenties, Tara read the tarot to pay her bills while forty-something Monica was someone who had never worked. Nor would she ever need to.

She was Tara's erstwhile client. Monica had come to seek counsel in Tara's tarot just three months ago. Back then, Monica's skeletal frame had quivered with anxiety. Her eyes had dark circles, bags and deep-seated grief. But just a quarter of a year had passed since, and seated in front of Tara was a composed, radiant Monica.

Gathering her bearings, Tara said, 'It is dangerous. You could get into a lot of trouble.'

Monica picked up a piece of sushi with her chopsticks.

'I don't see how. I am not cheating on anyone. On the contrary, my husband—sorry, I mean to-be-ex-husband—was cheating on me, right?' Saying this, she dipped the sushi in a thin puddle of piquant Kikkoman.

'But he is not just any man, don't you get it? He is a gangster, damn it. Those "*dishkyaon dishkyaon goli maron bheje mein*" types?'

'Until I met him, I had no clue what I was missing for twenty years of married life! With To-Be-Ex-Husband everything was *so* boring, Tara.' Saying this, she put the taut bundle in her mouth. Tara stared at Monica as she enjoyed her bite.

'Is he married?' she asked.

Monica had her mouth full and could not speak. However, she nodded. Yes. And while Tara thought she could not be shocked any further, Monica put her thumb on her little finger and raised the index, middle and ring in that specific order.

'Thrice?!' squealed Tara.

The din in the room hushed for a beat. Monica continued enjoying her bite. After the sushi was demolished inside her mouth, she pursed her lips and licked her teeth with zen-like mindfulness, hoping no morsel was stuck in between. Next, she reached out for a glass of water but Tara stopped her hand with a light slap.

'Three times?!'

'No, three wives. Same time.'

Tara stared at her friend.

'Yes, Altaf Sheikh has three wives,' she stated emphatically and added, 'each in a different decade of life. The eldest is around my age, the second must be in her thirties, and the youngest in her late twenties, just like you, Tara.'

'Monica...'

'Yes?'

'I...I...don't know what to say... Don't you think you are doing something wrong?'

'I am the single woman here. He is married. It should be his lookout, *na*? And besides, no one thought of me when To-Be-Ex-Husband was busy screwing his Sales VP, now fiancée, right?'

'It is bad karma,' said Tara, shaking her head from one side to the other.

'But the sex is exceptional!' piped up Monica and called for the bill.

As the two glided towards the door of the restaurant, they heard thundering laughter from a nearby table. Then the laughter stopped abruptly, prompting Monica to turn and take a look. The eight ladies seated there stared at Monica. And she stared back. They had been friends for two decades. They used to be a team: the wealthy sisterhood who ate small bites in public and binged on biryani in private. And together they'd purge it out as well for fear of getting fat. Apart from wealth and status, they were united in their fears too: getting fat, and losing their husbands to the charms of another woman.

Now that Monica was not 'Mrs Singh', her status had dipped amongst them. She may still be wealthy, but she was no longer 'one of them'. Why? Because they chose to quietly side with the decisions made by their respective husbands, Monica's to-be-ex-husband's school buddies.

The last time Monica had tried to contact the wives was three months ago. But after her separation, they simply did not take her calls. *After all, it's not the same anymore*, they thought.

Now, uncertain of how to react, they looked at her. Then, at each other, fumbling for words. For her part, Monica folded her hands and waited patiently. Intimidated by the hostility of the rich, Tara, who was going to get dropped at the station to catch the local for her home in the far-flung suburb these women would call Candy Valley (Kandivali), stood a few steps behind.

One of them spoke up. Feigning concern, she asked, 'Monica? Hope you are fine? Do you have thyroid?'

Monica shook her head no.

'You look like you have piled on a few pounds.' Saying this, she looked at her pack, who nodded back, acknowledging the observation.

But that did not deter Monica. She continued to smile beatifically. And then, without thinking, words of wisdom involuntarily spewed forth.

'That is because I have been having mind-boggling orgasmic sex. He makes me come multiple times, each time, every time. I scream in crazy ecstasy. I am busy screwing unlike all of you who snoop on your husbands to find out who *they* have been sleeping with. Because who better than me to know that none of you get much action? Bye, babies. I got to meet and mate. And after I am done, we both shall share a meal. Nalli nihari and boti kebab!' her voice thundered.

Announcing her post-coital Mughlai meal plan in one of the city's most exclusive Japanese restaurants, Monica glided away from the shocked bunch. Then, as an afterthought, she swooped right back into the fold. Staring at the woman who had mentioned her weight gain, Monica parted her palms wide and bringing her face closer said, 'It is that long, Rashmi.' She then picked up an oblong sashimi roll from Rashmi's plate and twirling it around said, 'Unlike your husband's *nunu*.'

Not knowing where to look, the rest of the ladies started swivelling their necks like a parliament of owls. Tossing the sashimi back on the plate, Monica belched into her victim's face. Wordless, Rashmi cringed.

The posse then stared at her as she sashayed away, holding onto her camera bag as if it was as precious as a monogrammed limited edition LV sling. She looked filled in—with poise, confidence and assertiveness. Like she did not have a care in the world. And that was so alluring. She was a far cry from the sheepish, gaunt Monica who always listened, never the one to talk.

How did she change so drastically after her separation?

And most importantly, who was this guy giving her multiple orgasms each time, every time?

What happened to 'their' Monica? Her former 'friends' began to wonder.

Thinking hard, one of them snapped up a bite of sashimi between her chopsticks. Just as she was about to put it in her mouth, her eyes slanted towards Rashmi. Quietly, she put the piece back on its plate. The table had now lost its appetite for the Japanese delicacy.

1

Three months ago: Powder Room.
The Royal Bombay Yacht Club, Colaba.

*M*onica looked at her reflection and did not like it. A drawn face, tired from insomnia. Sunken eyes on the verge of tears. The best foundation and concealer could not hide the dark bulging bags underneath. Putting her hand on her lower abdomen, she then moved it up to her solar plexus and pressed it firmly. There it was, a gnawing gut, as if aware of impending doom but uncertain as to what exactly the problem was.

Monica then stared at her face, pursed her lips and whispered, '*Baanjh*.'

Blood curdled in her veins as tears welled up in her sunken eyes.

'Baanjh.' The blasphemous word for women who cannot conceive quivered through yet again.

'Baanjh,' she repeated as Rashmi, aka Mrs Nunu, walked in *tok-tok*, her Louboutin heels clacking on the marble floor of the club.

'Eeew! What did you just say?'

'I just repeated what I overheard this morning. Raghu's

phone was in speaker mode when he was talking to his mother. She said it. He put the phone off speaker mode just as I entered the room. But the cursed word did not escape me.'

'Really?'

'I could not get the entire phone conversation, but it seemed as if she was agreeing with him. It seemed like he was asking for approval.'

Rashmi looked into the mirror to check on her red lipstick. It had smudged a bit at the corners.

'These men are such idiots. Balding, ageing, but no, they still need *Mummy-ji's* approval. Nunu is the same.'

Hearing the secret nickname for Rashmi's husband (coined by a sexually frustrated Rashmi herself), a small smile flitted across Monica's sad face.

'So glad the mention of Nunu made you smile. He is of no use otherwise. And c'mon now, we have work to do. This club serves the best dhansak–rice in the world, damn it, but I just Googled. Mutton dhansak has 415 calories. Plus, we had brown rice. That is another 396. We don't want to be getting fat now.'

Saying this, she headed to the loo, pulling Monica by her skeletal arm. Next, both the lunching ladies dug their acrylic talons deep into their mouths and expunged the world-famous mutton dhansak from the Royal Bombay Yacht Club.

⌒

'I feel something terrible is going to happen,' Monica mumbled as they walked down the imperial corridors towards her car.

Rashmi asked, 'You have been feeling this for long, na? Is it that same one, that sales girl Raghu is screwing?'

'Vice president sales,' corrected Monica. The valet opened

the door of the Bentley and Monica took the driver's seat. She rolled down the window and, giving him a currency note, looked at him and said a quick thank-you. Strapping her seat belt she added, 'From Jamnalal Bajaj Institute of Management.'

She then tapped her finger on her temple. 'The woman has brains. She tripled business for him in the two years that she has been with the company. Raghu is smitten by her. Calls her his *Luckshmi. L-U-C-K-shmi.*' Saying this, she rolled her Bentley into the crowded roads and the cacophony of Mumbai.

‿

As her car drove down Haji Bunder, Rashmi asked Monica, 'Do you think you and Raghu have fallen apart because you don't have kids?'

Monica heaved as she pointed to a looming gate that gradually came into view: Suri Charities. It belonged to Monica, from her parents and forefathers. It was a sprawling ancestral estate which housed several aids. An adoption home, a home for the destitute, a cancer hospice for the terminally ill, an experimental theatre and a free primary school for the underprivileged—it was a haven of goodness. A green sea-facing oasis bang in the heart of Mumbai, it had been her great grandfather's land. In 1932 the governor of Bombay Presidency had inaugurated the property for the welfare of the poor and destitute.

'I mentioned adopting a child from the adoption agency on our estate. But no. Some crap called "*humara khoon*". And it is not just Raghu or his mother. My parents also think that a child must be borne of bloodline.'

'Do you miss having a child, Monica?'

'Not at all. I am absolutely okay not having one. But

the constant pressure of my family's unfulfilled expectations of me is choking my life. Yaar, I have done all the things everyone asked of me. Now if I can't have a child, is it my bloody fault? Am I no longer good enough for my people? I am fed up yaar!'

A beat. The car rumbled on. Rashmi touched Monica's arm and she took a deep breath.

'All I want is to be accepted for who I am. That's it. Just the way I am. Is that asking for too much?'

Rashmi stared at Monica. Such existential crises were not her cup of tea.

2

*M*onica rang the doorbell of her palatial duplex. The door opened slightly and she saw her loyal attendant, Manda, come into view. Monica smiled. Manda's presence was always reassuring.

But not at the moment. Manda looked petrified.

'What's the matter, Manda? In my absence did you call your boyfriend over?' teased Monica and stepped into the apartment.

And then, stopped in her tracks. Husband Raghu was standing as if waiting for her to arrive. Monica looked at the dial of the oversized Rolex on her bony wrist.

It was 4.00 in the afternoon, unusually early for her workaholic husband to be home. He smiled at her tentatively. And as she stepped closer, Raghu's 'Luckshmi' came into view!

She was *so* pregnant!

'Co-cong…ratulations,' mumbled Monica and added with a brief smile of relief, 'I did not know you were married.'

'I am not,' said the sheepish VP Sales and slowly turned to look at Raghu.

Monica paused to stare. Pointing at the bump, she looked at Raghu. He shrugged helplessly as if it was not his fault.

Monica opened her mouth to say something, but just

then she heard wailing. Looking to the side, she saw two similarly dressed toddlers bobbing their bodies and screaming away despite two uniformed nannies trying their best to calm them down.

Monica turned to Raghu. When he nodded yes, Monica thought she was going to faint.

Suddenly her palatial sanitized home was brimming with illegitimate twin toddlers and the 'other' woman who had been impregnated by her husband. She looked at Raghu, who crossed his arms and stood staring at her. Finally, things fell into place. Since joining his company two years ago, she had not only tripled his sales but given him three kids as well!

And just then she remembered the word from that morning—baanjh. *Fucking bitch*, Monica cursed her mother-in-law silently.

Which meant that for the sake of the bloodline, DJ-laden raucous birthday parties which served cheese-chutney sandwiches and oily mini-pizzas, and cranky kids who'd grow up to be ungrateful teenagers, Raghu wanted his mother's approval to dump Monica and marry his mistress who popped ova like a popcorn vending machine.

And to assuage his guilt, he was promising Monica a similar lifestyle to the one she was leading. A tastefully furnished luxury apartment in Bandstand, a uniformed staff, two high-end cars and a generous alimony would be available for her soon. All this was mentioned in the separation papers that he was now handing to her.

'In a great big rush to leave me, Raghu?' asked Monica and turned to the stairway. She did not take the papers.

Then she stepped up the stairs. Slowly. Monica had known that something was amiss ever since Raghu had started speaking about his new business development manager in conversations with the buddies. Clearly he had a thing for her. But this sales señorita was not the first. In twenty years of marriage, Raghu had had plenty of dalliances, albeit ignored by Monica. *There's no point in shaking the cart*, she had thought. For that is how one was taught to think. *Ignore the dalliances of a man. After all, men will be men. And while they have their fun outside, no one leaves the wife*—that was the rule.

Once, as a child, she had overheard a piss-drunk bawdy *mamaji* slur out loud at a family party, '*Array voh thakur hi kaisa, joh nachne wali ke paas nahi jaata ho?* What kind of a thakur is he who does not have a nautch girl dancing to his tunes?' Everyone had had a good laugh, even the women. So, like a well-taught student, Monica swept Raghu's liaisons under the carpet. Despite it bothering her, both husband and wife played their parts well.

Until today, however, she had been clueless about the illegitimate bloodline Raghu was spawning. *Not one but three!*

What felt worse was her inability to bear an offspring. In the twenty years of their marriage, she had gone through the horrors of attempting reproduction several times. Rushed, loveless coitus in the 'window period', lying on her back and sticking her legs upright on the wall in the hope that a single sperm hit bullseye, artificial insemination, chanting *jaaps*, keeping *vrats*, attending *mata ki chowkis*, feeding temple ants with dough dipped in sugar on Wednesdays—nothing had worked in her favour. At first, Raghu had been encouraging… but when time catapulted her from the twenties to the late thirties, his hopes started to dwindle.

For her part, Monica had suggested adoption from the centre built on their Haji Bunder plot. The family had dismissed the idea. She could not understand how the bloodline made a difference in the joy of raising a child. *Aren't all children a reflection of God's desire?* she thought, but never had the courage to voice her opinion.

Raghu had not asked her to leave outright. He did not have the guts. But staying was pointless. It would only hurt to see him openly shower love and care on 'Luckshmi'. Their marriage had failed. Monica was too dignified to fight for the affections of a man who did not want her. Furthermore, she blamed herself. *If we had a child, none of this would have happened*, she thought. After all, both Raghu and Monica came from the same rarefied socio-economic strata of society.

Her inability to procreate was soon going to be her biggest blessing. Of course, Monica Singh did not think so. Not at the moment.

In the vast designer bedroom now, she called for Manda. Then, matter-of-factly, sans expression, asked her to bring out the Louis Vuitton trunks. And to start packing her effects: books, clothes and shoes.

Just then, the dignified lull gave way and an avalanche of tears gushed forth. Charting down a gaunt face, they cascaded to the marble floor. She had no power to stop the flow despite cupping her eyes with bejewelled fingers topped with shimmering acrylic nails.

Carb-deprived forty-year-old Monica cried copiously. She dropped her head into the cups of her bony hands.

A much-worried Manda hid her concern. Madam was always kind and respectful to her, unlike her previous employers who treated their staff like filth. Manda impassively continued to pack all the belongings her Madam had in their twenty-year-old conjugal sea-facing duplex. She wanted to reach out but thought it to be prudent not to involve herself in the complexities of the rich.

Monica dialled her mother. Then she cut the call because this was not the subject for a phone conversation. Her entire family had to know about the horror that had ensued. *Surely, they'd understand…*she thought.

Teary-eyed, Monica instructed Manda to continue packing. It was just a matter of time before her efficient Manda would have her belongings dispatched. Now, she had to make swift headway to the main door, deliberately avoiding unpleasant sights along the route.

At the threshold of her bedroom, Monica looked back at what had been her haven. A fresh burst of tears spewed forth.

Wiping them with her palms she tiptoed down the stairs. Manda followed. She wanted to ensure Madam was okay.

Now, To-Be-Ex-Husband Raghu stood up from the sofa. It was not just any sofa. It was a Boca Do Lobo—an intricately carved limited-edition exclusive luxury piece flown in from Portugal on the occasion of their wedding anniversary. The twins were scratching the carvings now. Monica wanted to stop them and even stared longer than was necessary. But the irritable pregnant mistress continued to fuss over the twins without asking them to stop. Perhaps that was her excuse to not look at Monica.

To-Be-Ex-Husband handed her the papers. Renewed tears gushed forth as Monica meticulously read them. She was one of those who read everything before signing. The husband had been decent about the separation. She would have a similar lifestyle to the one she currently had, except he would not be a part of it.

'Is there anything else you want from here?' he asked.

Monica looked around the house. Her gaze stopped at Manda.

'Please relieve Manda for me. She is the only one I cannot live without,' said Monica, as she continued to read. And then when she was finished, Monica paused. Broke into tears yet again as she signed on the dotted line. Her inked signature drowned in pelting teardrops. She felt sorry for herself, thinking about how lucky the mistress was.

On the other hand, the mistress was jealous of Monica now. Because more attractive than a pretty face or a toned body was freedom. Monica was wealthy and would always be. But now she'd have her freedom from all trappings. That was so attractive. Tied down with wailing twins, post-partum depression and other pregnancy issues, the mistress actually wished she was footloose. Just like she had been two years ago before she joined Raghu's company. Socially ambitious, she had wanted to change her address from Bhayandar to Bandra. Clearly, her love for a palatial duplex in Pali Hill was far greater than the attraction she had coaxed out of herself for Raghu.

'Manda, pack my belongings and send them to Suri Manor.'

'Yes, Madam.'

'Bye, Manda, see you soon.'

And then, without looking at To-Be-Ex-Husband or his mistress, Monica shut the door.

3

For those who are not well-versed with the geopolitics of Mumbai, here is one important piece of information: despite being an island city flanked by the Arabian Sea, four hills form the city's stratosphere. In the hamlets of Malabar Hill, Altamount Road, Pali Hill and Mount Mary reside the city's rich, richer and richest.

Now, Monica's Bentley glided from To-Be-Ex-Husband's penthouse on Pali Hill into Papa Suri's sprawling bungalow on Mount Mary. Papa Suri lived with Mumma Suri, Bhai Suri and Bhabhi Suri in a spacious manor. There was plenty of room in their hearts as well, or so she thought.

Stepping out of her elegant machine, Monica began to walk down the manicured lawns she had played in as a little girl. Seconds later, her mother and sister-in-law came into view. Faint mumbling could be heard from them. Seated at the coffee table set in the farthest corner of the green patch, the ladies were sipping their evening whiskey. The Macallan, Glenlivet and Bruichladdich were laid out on the trolley soon after the sun had splattered across the horizon of the Arabian Sea. Once he was back from work, which would be any time now, her sixty-five-year-old dapper Papa Suri would join the family ritual.

When a svelte Mumma Suri came into sharp focus, Monica hastened her steps and was soon running towards her. The sixty-year-old with blow-dried hair and a French manicure stood up seeing her teary-eyed daughter sprint and now fling herself into her arms. Monica started to howl out loud.

As Mumma Suri patted her daughter, she continued her conversation with Bhabhi Suri, 'But don't you think that Kavita was a little too overdressed for her own mother's *chautha?*'

'I don't think so, Mummy-ji. Maybe it was an ode to her late mother. After all, Vinny Aunty was a famous designer, *nahi?*' said Bhabhi Suri as she took a large gulp of the golden liquid.

'World famous in Trotter's Club,' Mumma Suri sniggered.

'*Achcha*, Mummy-ji, from tomorrow I am on a liquid diet,' announced Bhabhi Suri.

'Aren't you now, *beta?*' and Mumma Suri sniggered yet again.

Monica looked up deadpan. 'Mumma? When are you going to ask me what's wrong?'

A smug smile curled up Mumma Suri's face. 'Beta, there is no problem in this world that a drink cannot solve. Come, let me fix you a drink.' Saying this, Mumma Suri poured a large volume of the Glenlivet for Monica.

'There is nothing to solve. I have signed the divorce papers,' confessed Monica as she took a seat.

The two ladies froze.

'Stand up!' Mumma Suri demanded.

'What?' Monica stared at her mother for a beat but, under her firm gaze, got up. Involuntarily, fingers entangled into one another, then her head stooped low, and Monica resembled a reprimanded school girl.

Monica opened her mouth to speak. But she was asked to stop yet again. This time it was her sister-in-law, Bhabhi Suri.

'Didi, one minute. I need a refill first,' she said and scuttled to the trolley. Hastily pouring an extra-large volume of the golden liquid she explained, 'You see, I am taking it dry from tomorrow.' Then taking a sip, she added, 'Please. Continue, Didi.'

⌒

'How did you sign the papers? Tell me, just tell me how?!' her father bellowed as he fixed his third large peg of the Macallan.

An hour later, rooted to the spot, Monica was still as a dartboard. Taunts from her family pierced through her like tiny sharp missiles. But unlike the rules of dart where competing players get three turns at a time, her family attacked her in unison:

'Couldn't you check with one of us?'

'Where are your brains?'

'We could have consulted with a good lawyer. You know Tony, Hasina and I go back a long way, don't you now? Uncle R. Jay and your *nanaji* were in school together in Shikarpur.'

'Didi? Why did you not call me?'

'Can't you get one thing right?'

'What am I going to say to my *taash* friends?'

'Didi? You could have spoken to me first.'

And then came the one that hit the bullseye:

'What do I say to my squash buddies at the club? Neither can my daughter bear a child, nor is she capable of sustaining a marriage made in heaven?!'

Ouch!

Everyone stopped and stared at Papa Suri. Monica realized that not one of them had asked her how she was doing. How she felt after her husband's betrayal. Nobody cared. All they did was blame her. It was pointless being in their midst.

'Excuse me. I am exhausted. I will use the guest room till my flat is ready,' saying this she started to walk away.

'Beta…?' she heard her father's voice soften. Thinking he was going to apologize, she turned, all set to make amends.

'Papa…I understand your pain but—' she paused mid-sentence as her father raised his palm to stop her from speaking.

'Could you please not use the club? Everyone knows me there. Just stay away. I could buy you a membership at MCA if you wish but stay away from Trotter's, please. People will get to know and eventually gossip, but you being there will just make it worse for the rest of us.'

Monica nodded and turned around. As she walked away, there was another burst of tears. Involuntarily she started to run towards the porch and entered the bungalow. One male uniformed staff member was fixing the bed in the guest room. Without caring about propriety, she threw herself on the bed. The man flew away for the fear of getting caught in Baby-ji's room.

Her head was pounding. She needed someone. Someone who would be on her side. Monica dialled Rashmi.

∼

A glum Rashmi stared at Nunu as he admired his short squat frame in the mirror. He was getting dressed for the Trench Night. The Trench was an open secret. It was held in the basement of Nunu's two-storey bungalow. Nunu's real name was Manav Khanduja. The scion of a textile magnate, Nunu wanted to diversify into high fashion. However, due to a lack of basic discipline and foresight, and an unhealthy lure for all things glamorous, Nunu failed miserably. Egotistical due to a privileged childhood, he was too proud to go back into the family business. Besides, his father had better sense than to ask the prodigal son to rejoin the fold. Selling his flagging set-up for a pricey amount, Nunu then devoted his life to debauchery. He offered the finest cocaine, LSD and MDMA in the elite social soirées and media shindigs he hosted.

But the Trench was another universe. Hidden from the world, the Trench was infamous in circles that could afford his dope. It was not just the drugs and alcohol. Gorgeous, lanky, semi-naked struggling models and starlets added their dose of youth and glamour. Moreover, they charged by the hour at this men's-only shindig. Many young twenty-somethings found sugar daddies to eventually pay for their airfare, perfume, make-up, clothes, bags and shoes at this debauched watering hole.

Respective wives were strictly not allowed. And Rashmi hated Nunu even more when he hosted the Trench.

Now, both husband and wife slanted their gazes at the display of Rashmi's ringing mobile.

Nunu shrugged. 'You need to cut ties with her. After all, Raghu is my friend and that's how you and Monica, or, for that matter, your entire bunch know each other. The wives of us boys.'

Rashmi continued to glare at Nunu.

∽

Alone now, Monica dug her head into the pillow and screamed. The freshly covered muslin casing was soon damp with a mixture of tears, saliva and snot. Monica cried and cried till she could cry no more. When she finally went off to sleep, the black sky was just shifting into the deepest hue of purple.

∽

Nobody in the Suri family could sleep well that night. In fact, they had not been sleeping well for months now. Monica did not know that her separation only added to their misery.

The Suris, real estate moguls, were a generous lot. They had a special affection for the poor. They treated them as equals. *We are equal, so yours is mine and mine is also mine,* was their motto. They did not have business accounts with nationalized banks. Instead, the father–son duo held dubious accounts with a small cooperative bank whose other account holders were simple administrative staff, house-help and chauffeurs. This was done to build large-scale lower-income group housing in the far-flung eastern suburbs of the city, again in the interest of the poor.

After getting 200-odd crores, at first the Suris applied the cardinal rule of the rich—pay yourself first. So, they bought themselves a fleet of high-end cars, yachts and holiday homes. Next, they extended their generosity to others from their ilk: business tycoons, powerful politicians, top cops, cricket stars, Bollywood A-listers and media giants.

Handcrafted limited-edition jewellery and designer wardrobes were curated for every Suri shindig. From 'surprise' birthday parties for superstars to Iftar evenings for politicians, from mata ki chowkis for the business head honchos to Halloween parties for star kids and their mommies—lavish soirées were hosted on the ancestral Suri Manor by the sea.

Guests were showered with exclusive gifts as if it was confetti. The lowest in the guest hierarchy, lifestyle reporters who wrote about them in fashion magazines and the after-hours section of newspapers, were often bestowed with 'inexpensive nuggets' like perfumes, make-up or a bottle of wine depending upon the network and the reporter's pecking order in it.

And while basking in luxury they did not forget the poor, of course. In their concern for the needs of the poor, instead of constructing twenty-storey buildings, they constructed thirty. That way, more poor people would make them richer by buying their generously constructed pint-sized rooms.

Luck ran its princely course. Glamorous soirées on holiday estates, yacht parties for fashionistas, book launches for friends—the Suris were the toast of the town. A beacon of how a family should be—wealthy, powerful and glamorous. Meanwhile, the working class got bank loans and booked apartments in Suri Housing in the hope of improving their standard of living. Everyone was happy.

But after running an extensive triathlon for a little less than a decade, eventually luck began to lose steam. The Suri Housing Project was stalled by the Bombay High Court due to illegal construction. Bank loans were unpaid and interests were mounting by the second. Soon the father–son duo, Dharam and Abhay Suri, were on the radar of the Economic Offences Wing and Enforcement Directorate, two government bodies that kept an eye out for economic frauds. The Suris were on their LOC, Look-Out Circular.

The family started to feel the pressure. Of late, Papa and Mumma Suri had been denied permission to leave the country. No apparent reason was given by the immigration officer at the Mumbai airport. Though it bothered them, they knew that it was a matter of time…they'd be off the radar soon. After all, all the powerful people—politicians, cops, lawyers, reporters—were their friends. And the Suris continued to live the good life, cushioned in the myth that bad things happened only to others.

'What is the worst that could happen to us?' asked Bhabhi Suri, as an oversized and inebriated Abhay, Bhai Suri, waddled in, in the wee hours of the morning.

'We will be disgraced. All our properties will be sealed. Our fleet of cars and yachts will be sold. Your clothes and jewellery will be auctioned,' slurred a numb Abhay as he slumped into bed.

'Are you sure there is nothing we can do? Abhay? Anything, anything we could do to save ourselves?' Bhabhi Suri pleaded.

Abhay thought hard. Really hard. And then he passed out.

4

*W*hen he woke up the next day, Abhay Suri found himself smiling after months. A hurried shower was followed by hastily wearing a fresh pair of jeans and a T-shirt. There was a new-found agility as he slipped his clunky feet into his suede Stefano Bemers.

On his way out at 7.30 a.m., he passed by the lavishly laid breakfast table. The senior Suris had always been early risers. Mumma Suri was monitoring the layout: an oversized platter of chopped fruit, a tall jug of freshly squeezed orange juice, a smattering of liver fry and cold cuts and boiled eggs. Then she laid out the bread, secretly hoping no one would have it.

Abhay pecked his mother. Then grabbed a dry toast. Next, he poured himself black coffee, some of which spilt on the table. Ignoring the mess, he reached out for the white sugar.

'Come on now. You must eat well, Abhay,' his mother fussed over her *ladlaa* beta. 'You put on weight because you don't eat healthy.'

'I am late for office, Mom. I have to get us out of this mess.' Saying this he pecked Mumma Suri on the cheek and smiled at Papa Suri, who was back from his game of squash.

'And will you enlighten us regarding your ingenious plan?' asked Papa Suri as he took his first sip of juice.

Abhay did not miss the sarcasm. However, he smiled. For his parents were unaware of a certain gold mine. He too had remembered just this morning.

The Suris were so wealthy that they had forgotten their hidden treasures stashed away in the south of Mumbai. When Abhay mentioned their Haji Bunder plot, Papa Suri sat down and Mumma put her hand to her mouth, which had involuntarily fallen open. She sat down with a thud.

'We make nothing out of that land. It is wasted on the sick and the destitute,' said Abhay.

But now the Suris would be destitute and poor if they did not repay their loans. It being an ancestral parcel of land in the heart of sea-facing South Bombay, they could easily sell it and repay their bad debts.

Now a uniformed attendant followed Abhay with a tray of black coffee, a quarter plate and a napkin. Abhay wolfed down his toast as he walked to the porch.

At a distance, he saw Monica stroll away slowly by the edge of the lawn. Abhay turned to the attendant and scarfed down another large portion of toast. As soon as his chauffeur-driven car slid in, he shoved the remaining wedge of uneaten bread in his mouth and got inside. Next, he opened his laptop. Talking to his sister now would waste at least half an hour. And time was money. He had to work fast before law enforcers arrested them.

Monica heard the roar of the A-Class Mercedes. She turned to look in the direction of the sound. Her younger brother Abhay was staring at the screen of his laptop when his car whizzed by.

༄

Abhay worked swiftly. A buyer was willing and Abhay's lawyers prepared papers for the sale of the plot. Simultaneously, goons were hired to start making life miserable for inmates and social workers. They harassed the children and elderly. Signatures relinquishing rights over the land were signed at lightning pace as social workers were held at gunpoint. Everything was done! Just the last bit was left and the Suris would soon be out of trouble.

Being an ancestral property, it belonged to all the Suris. This included Monica. Her signature was mandatory for the final sale of land. She, however, was oblivious to the murky state of affairs. Up till now, they had kept her in the dark about their distress.

When Papa Suri called for Monica, she felt a bit better. Perhaps he wanted to make amends with his daughter. Perhaps he had realized his mistake and now the family would warm up to her, thought Monica.

But, at the dining table, when Papa Suri shoved under her nose the last page of the transfer document demanding Monica's signature, she was on her guard. As always, she read the document carefully and realized her family's intentions to sell their ancestral plot to a buyer who would make a luxury market city on their estate.

Monica stared at her father. 'Where will the children go? The orphans? The elderly? What happens to them, Papa?'

'Don't ask questions; you just sign the papers, okay?'

'No? Why? It is not right,' defied Monica.

Papa Suri was shocked. Monica had always yielded to his wishes, no questions asked.

'You want us to go to jail?' he asked.

Monica stared at her father. She was clueless. And that's

when Mumma Suri told Monica about their financial woes.

'This is the only way out, Monica,' said her mother without an iota of guilt.

'Where will the children go, Mom? You taught us to be considerate. To feed the poor, to help the underprivileged. *Kar bhala toh ho bhala*, you used to say to me. Perhaps all the good done to us is because of that land.'

'You care more about orphans than your own family?' reprimanded Mumma Suri.

Papa Suri held his daughter by her arm and squeezed it. 'Sign. Or I will kill you. I know how to make people sign, lady.'

Before Monica could react, Abhay intervened and pulled his father away from her. *Thank God, at least my brother is on my side!* thought Monica.

'Dad, you don't want the Crime Branch hounding you for threatening a murder now. ED is already a handful.'

Papa Suri agreed.

'Let's forge her signature then,' he said in front of her.

Abhay nodded in disgust. 'Papa, please shut up and let me handle this.' Then he looked at Monica. 'Didi, you don't want to sign, we cannot force you. But clearly we are not important, we know now. We will figure a way to get out of this. Thank you, Didi.'

A numb Monica stared at her family as they walked away from her. Was this really happening to her? Or was this just a nightmare that she was going through and would soon wake up from? What was going on?

5

*O*ver the next couple of days, life slipped by. Papa and Mumma Suri were hosting a 'small' soirée at the manor, which she only found out about when caterers and light men started to set up in the afternoon. Neither Bhabhi nor Mumma asked her to join them for their Tuesday taash sessions despite knowing that there was free time and no one to talk to.

Monica called Rashmi yet again. This time she answered.

'Rashmi!' Monica cried and added, 'You have no idea—'

'I know, Monica. I heard.'

Monica froze for a beat.

'And you did not think of calling me, Rashmi?'

'Monica, you know how it works. I mean, we wouldn't be friends had it not been for our husbands.'

'Oh, so now you will be Luckshmi's best friend?'

'Monica…'

'Rashmi…'

'Yes?'

'Go fuck yourself, bitch!' Saying this, Monica hung up. Did Monica not mean anything to anyone? What kind of relationships were these? Despite family and friends, there was no one to turn to! And while she was going through the worst time of her life, everyone else seemed to move on happily without her. Dark, unutterable loneliness snaked around her, and that's when the first cracks started to form.

For days on end, she would be in front of the TV. Just staring. Without changing out of her pyjamas, she would just sit and stare. All day long, web series, news, soap operas and films were binged to the point of apathy. Thankfully Monica was only a social drinker; else she would have turned into a full-blown alcoholic gazing emptily at the television screen.

One night, Monica startled out of bed. Her savage shrieks pierced through the stillness. The entire family woke up thinking there was a murder in their manor. Abhay and his parents ran to Monica.

Crouched on the bed, she was screaming away. Mumma Suri shook Monica.

'What is the matter with you?'

Monica dug her head in the folds of her limbs and shook it like an angry bull.

'Look up!' Mumma Suri yelled. Monica slowly turned to look up. Staring at her mother, she screamed yet again.

Unsure of how to react responsibly, Papa Suri was motionless. On the other hand, believing that his sister was under the spell of momentary madness, Abhay took the bottle of water from the bedside, poured some in his hand and splashed it on her face. The chilled splatter seemed to work and she stopped shrieking. Encouraged, Abhay poured the entire bottle on her crown. Monica started to inhale—long, deep and laborious breaths.

'I am going crazy. I can't breathe,' she finally managed to mutter.

'What?!' asked Abhay Suri.

'Nonsense,' declared Mumma Suri.

'Are you smoking up by any chance?' Uttering rubbish amid trauma came naturally to Papa Suri.

'Papa, no one screams after smoking up. They are relaxed,' said Abhay calmly.

'How do you know? Abhay? Have you tried drugs by any chance? I am telling you that this is the one thing that won't be tolerated in this house. No drugs,' warned Papa Suri.

Mumma Suri snapped. 'My children don't do drugs. I have raised them well.'

Monica stared at the three of them. Her topic was flung out of the window.

'Then what happened to her?' asked an indignant Papa Suri. 'Bloody idiot, she is of no use! Neither to her husband, nor to us!'

Ah! They were back to focusing on her now! Suddenly, from a victim, she had morphed into an angry lunatic.

'What the *fuck* is wrong with you, Papa? Why the hell are you so mean? What have I done wrong? My husband screwed around behind my back, he got a staff member pregnant and you blame me? You and Abhay messed up with the business. Want to get poor children out on the street because of your greed… What have I done that is so wrong, Papa? Am I not doing what is right? Where is your conscience, everyone? What the *fuck* is wrong with you all?'

Papa Suri stared at Monica. Then looked at his wife and said, 'Is this the way you have raised her? To talk to elders like that. Using the F-word?' Mumma Suri looked at Monica and hung her head in shame. He turned to Monica, 'Because of you, we could all go to jail…do you understand? I have no sympathy for you. Just get out of my sight!'

Monica cupped her mouth with her hands. She could not

believe how hard-hearted Papa was or what an insensitive woman her mother had become. And then she slowly moved to the corner of the room and started shrieking yet again. Loudly. Abhay and his parents shut their ears.

And at that moment, amid the deafening shrieks that shook the manor, Abhay knew it was time to seek medical intervention.

∽

Hours later, Doctor Sahay poked an injection into Monica's bony limb.

'This is just post-separation anxiety, Madam. So many changes in your life…it happens. You will feel much calmer now.' The doctor smiled at Monica and pulled the injection out.

Too tired to smile, she acknowledged him with a long blink. Then, while administering the second injection the doctor suggested, 'Perhaps you could take up a new hobby or register for some classes? It will take your mind off things, you know. Goodnight. Sleep well now, Madam,' said the soft-spoken doctor and turned off the light in her bedroom. Within a beat, Monica slipped into a much-needed restful sleep.

When she woke up the next day, it was already 3.00 in the afternoon. The twelve-hour long hard slumber was invigorating. Everything felt new. The room was dark. Monica drew the curtains and soaked her skeletal frame in the bright sunlight. A long and luxurious shower followed. Then, sliding into a pair of comfortable corduroy pants and a T-shirt, she resolved to go out into the world.

And do what, honey? Her inner critic reared its ugly head. Her inner critic had the raspy voice of her mother and looked like her father. *What is it that you will achieve that we haven't already?*

Photography, the softest whisper came from deep within. Quiet intuition was assertive and reassuring, much to her surprise.

As a young woman, Monica had always wanted to learn street photography. 'You are a princess, what will you do on the streets?' Mumma Suri had said. Very often, her choices were dismissed and decisions were tailor-made for her. She was encouraged to pursue humanities in a city college while Abhay was sent abroad after his Class XII board exams. She was only allowed to pursue a foreign education at the last standing finishing school in Switzerland, where she mingled with princesses and daughters of presidents and high-profile business owners. Monica enjoyed her brief independence. But it was the exposure to foreign cultures, a part of the curriculum in the finishing school, which livened her being.

Monica was aware that she was being engineered to be the trophy wife with the choicest taste. But she had a simple heart, because of which she sought meaning and beauty in a common person's every day. That she loved photography was evident from the Instagram handles she was following: Raghu Rai, Dayanita Singh, Sooni Taraporevala and many more. While her former friends would follow the Kardashians and Bollywood Wives, Monica sailed through the pictures created by the powerhouse Henri Cartier-Bresson, where a meaningful connection between a human being and their surroundings was made. She would be so engrossed that time stood still.

Perusing through images of people in their natural environment—now that's what she wanted to capture as well.

But where do I start?

She got up and walked to the banyan tree. One needed some shade to surf through one's phone. At first, Monica checked for photography classes.

As the sun started to set, Monica was mindful of the change of light. She looked up from her phone. Soon her family would be on the lawn having their evening drinks, and she did not want to be a part of it.

No darling, we don't want you to be a part of us, said her inner critic.

No, you selfish regressive morons. This time, we choose not to see you, replied her intuition. She felt euphoric as she walked out of the gates.

Mount Mary. This Church had given her such peace. On her extended trips abroad, she always missed the sights and sounds of Mumbai. And the first vision that came to her mind on foreign shores was Mount Mary. Every time she prayed, she lit eight candles, one for each member of her family plus one or two for her friends who might be in trouble. And Monica would pray fervently for her family and friends and almost always for a child. But in that instance, as the warmth of the burning candles enveloped her, she prayed for just two things: strength and guidance. Looking up at Our Lady of the Mount, she felt fortified.

6

A week later, Monica was in her first photography class. It was a fuss-free home tuition in an old Parsi *baug* situated in the heart of Girgaon, Central Mumbai. Her coach, Hormuzd Cawasji, was a respected retired photojournalist who did not care where his students came from. Instead, he was concerned about where they were going, in terms of frames, composition and light. Most of the students were college-going teenagers. If Monica had had a child in her early twenties, the offspring would be their age.

Right then walked in someone who looked like she was in her late twenties. 'Hello sir, I am Tara, the tarot card reader.'

'No,' replied Hormuzd Cawasji and continued, 'here none of you is anybody. You all will shut up and listen. No notes. Just listen. And no interruptions. For every question you may have, you will first look for the answer within and if you don't find the answer, ask after class is over. After class, I repeat. Got it?'

Monica smiled. She knew she was going to have a great time in Hormuzd Cawasji's class.

Despite dressing in her comfy non-branded T-shirt and stretch pants and wearing minimal make-up, Monica stood out from the other students. They struck furtive glances at her but that did not deter Monica. She was keen to learn a new craft.

And as Cawasji started to show slides and explain the hallmarks of a good photograph, a dull gnawing in her gut crept up sneakily. But Monica ignored it and focused on the lecture.

⁓

Monica and Tara started sitting next to one another. And Tara used her mobile as an excellent self-promotion tool. Her mobile display was a house of tarot. Her mobile cover had an image of a tarot card on it. In her notebook was the spread of tarot cards. Monica was amused looking at this tiny woman with straight hair who clearly had no interest in photography.

'Why do you come here?' asked Monica as they walked out of the precincts of the well-kept Shapur Baug.

'My boyfriend comes here, in the adjacent lane, for GMAT classes.'

'GMAT? How old is he?'

'Twenty-two,' she said and quickly added, 'I am twenty-eight. We live in Kandivali. In the same housing complex. So the train ride is a great way to be with him.'

'That's sweet.'

'Nothing sweet about it. I want to be with him as much as I can before he goes to Canada,' she said.

Monica saw teardrops forming in her eyes. Tara wiped them away. Monica felt drawn to this new, pint-sized friend.

'Hey girl, it's okay. You can always be in touch through video calls.'

'That won't happen. He will outgrow me.'

'Long-distance relationships do work out, you know.'

'This one won't.'

'How can you be so sure?'

'My tarot. It never lies.'

Monica stared as Tara walked ahead to greet her boyfriend. She felt pangs of grief when she saw the couple kiss and walk away holding hands. And then, yet again, the persistent gnawing in her gut reared its ugly head.

⁓

Days slipped into weeks. Monica had started taking pictures. Although Monica was immersed in her new pursuit, she was fully aware of the persistent fatigue and weakness. The gnawing in her gut had escalated to full-blown stomach ache. *Something is wrong*, her intuition said to her.

⁓

Luckily, the cards believed Monica when she took a train from Grant Road station all the way to Kandivali for a tarot reading. Very seriously, Tara looked at the spread and exclaimed, 'Oh my God. Death is around you.'

'What?!'

'Someone is trying to kill you.'

'Nonsense!'

Tara looked serious. She was no longer the airhead of Cawasji's class. This woman had command over her craft. She picked up a card and put it in front of Monica.

'This is the Devil card. And it is very close to home. Does someone in your family hate you?'

'They all do,' whispered Monica wryly, 'but they would not kill me.'

After all, her family was just angry because they were desperate to get out of the mess, that's all.

'My father cannot kill me.'

'No, it is a younger male energy. Do you have a brother? I get a male energy. He is very heavy.' Tara continued to speak staring at the cards. 'You are a wealthy woman. But betrayed by loved ones.'

Monica had no option but to believe her because no one knew her real identity. Rooted to the spot, it dawned on Monica that not only was she unwanted but she was also getting obliterated by her very own. Her spirit started to sink. When it reached rock bottom, it started scraping the surface to plunge further down.

However, the human spirit is a wilful thing; it unexpectedly floated in its spot and started to buoy its way up. It was going to survive.

At that moment, Monica vowed to get out of this mess. Any person's first option would be to go to the police. However, in her case, that was not an option as Papa and Abhay knew the rich and powerful of the country.

Tarot came to Monica's rescue yet again. Tara shut her eyes and asked Monica to pull another card with her right hand. Monica picked one and upturned it. The King of Swords.

'The Devil card is asking you to seek help from a dark force. See this, the Devil card signifies your problem with your family and the King of Swords will get you out of it. But at a price, of course.'

'Who is my King of Swords?'

Tara frowned as she stared at the cards and strummed her fingers on her lips. She then looked up to stare at Monica and stared down yet again. Then, biting her index finger, she asked tentatively, 'You have contacts with the underworld?'

Monica froze. After a beat, she mumbled, 'Are you out of your mind?'

'My cards don't lie. A gangster will help you out of the mess,' said Tara firmly. 'Can you at least try to find out, Monica?'

'Hello? Justdial? I need the numbers of five gangsters around me... Oh no, not Byinder or Candy Valley, please... *Haan Bandra chalega*, but Bandra West only, *haan*. However Sobo gangsters will be most preferred. After all, these Sobo gangsters always go international!' Monica's honey-toned voice was dripping with sarcasm.

But jokes apart, where was she going to find herself a gangster to save her life?

‿

At Bandra Fort, Monica tried to compose a frame of the setting sun. However, she found it hard to focus. Looking back at Tara she asked, 'Seriously, Tara. I am scared. I don't know where to find a gangster.'

Tara shrugged. 'Then don't find one.'

'But what about my life, then?'

'*Zindagi lambi nahi, badi honee chahiye.*' Life may not be long, but it better be large; tossing this evergreen line from the classic Hindi film *Anand*, Tara walked away.

‿

Due to a crazy traffic jam, Monica had to take a detour while going to Cawasji's class. Tara was seated next to her. Suddenly, a board came into view—Byculla Women's Correctional Facility.

'Look, that's the women's jail!' Tara said excitedly.

'Hey, will a lady gangster do?' asked Monica.
'The tarot said male energy. A dark, male energy.'

∽

Monica was scared to even type the word 'gangster' in her Google search engine. Perusing through the Mumbai Crime Files at the Centre for Education and Documentation in Colaba, Monica took a deep breath.

Then she scanned through newspapers of yesteryears. She read up on the city and its history with organized crime. There were many black-and-white photos: someone shot in an inter-gang tussle, a police encounter, a mugshot of an absconding don. And the byline of one photojournalist kept cropping up: Hormuzd Cawasji, Monica's photography teacher.

Monica closed the files. Her mind was running. She got up and marched towards the door. She passed the notice board of the centre, crammed with pamphlets. As an afterthought, Monica stopped in her tracks. She stepped back and peered at a notice on the board. A pamphlet—'AMATEUR PHOTOGRAPHY CONTEST: MUMBAI—THE ERA GONE BY'—was waiting for her. She peeled the pamphlet off and walked away.

∽

Monica waited for the class to disperse. After the last student had left, she went up to her professor.

'Sir,' she said and pushed the pamphlet on the table. Cawasji read it.

'Hmmm...the winning picture will be on the cover page of *National Geographic*, India. Do you think you are ready for a contest, Monica?'

'How will I know until I take my pictures, sir?'

'In that case, go for it.'

'Sir, apart from the old structures of the city, I want to capture the people...'

'What do you mean?'

'Like...you know...gangsters...'

'For "the era gone by"? Hmm... Most are dead. The ones alive are abroad. The ones who are in the city have retired.'

Monica squealed, 'Sir, I want someone from the city. It will be great to click him in his burrow. Who is this person, where did he come from, and where is he going?'

'It is better that you focus on the buildings and structures.'

'Of course I will, sir. But please share a number, na? I will see what I can get.'

Cawasji stared at Monica.

On the spur of the moment, she added drama to the state of affairs. 'This contest is very important for me, sir. If I win, apart from my picture on the cover page, I also get a paid internship with *National Geographic*! I have never had a career until now. But better late than never, sir.'

'One enthu-cutlet you are!' Saying this, he opened the bottom-most drawer of his table. It was crammed with old newspapers. From under the newspapers, he pulled out a tattered telephone diary and started leafing through its fragile yellowed pages.

⟍⟋

In her car, Monica swallowed the lump in her throat as she stared at the display of her mobile phone: ALTAF SHEIKH. Bracing herself, she punched in the digits yet again. And for the second time now, she put the phone away.

~

Surrounded by henchmen, forty-something Altaf Sheikh held court. With his chiselled nose, sharp cleft chin and cool green eyes, Altaf could have passed as a good-looking man, had it not been for the countless scars gashed across a dour countenance.

A police constable was at his feet, pleading.

'Sheikh Saab,' he addressed him out of respect and added, 'it has been four days. There is no water supply in my chawl. Please do something.'

Just then his mobile rang. Altaf reached for the phone but the call got cut, yet again. A tad miffed by the interference, he refocused on the business of the day.

'*Police chawl main paani nahi aa raha?*' Altaf was surprised that there was no water supply in a police chawl.

'Saab, I have made so many complaints to the Ward office. They don't respond.'

'*Chawl D-1 Ward ke under hai na?*' asked Altaf. The police constable nodded. Yes, the chawl was under the jurisdiction of the D-1 ward. Altaf looked at his henchmen. They stared back at him, confused.

Altaf's mobile rang again. Before he could answer, the call got cut.

Turning to his dim-witted cronies, Altaf gritted his teeth. He paused for a beat, hoping that those asses would get the message: to pick up the ward officer and bring him there. However, they kept waiting until Altaf had to yell his instructions out loud, '*Abbey Gadhon! Ward officer ko utha ke leke aao!*'

That's when his henchmen scurried away to kidnap the D-1 Ward officer. Altaf assured the police constable that his work would be done. The grateful man folded his hands in a namaste. Just then Altaf's phone rang. But Altaf ignored his ringing mobile because there was something very important he had to say to the constable. Altaf had to give his word. Assure the constable that the work would be done. And once it was, he had to ask the constable's chawl dwellers to vote for him, Sheikh Saab.

'*Sheikh ki zubaan hai. Kaam ho jayega. Chawl waalon ko bol dena. Vote phor Sheikh Saab.*'

The constable readily agreed. 'Who will not vote for you, Saab?'

Altaf grinned. '*Chal nikal. Pehle ticket toh aane do.*'

Altaf was waiting to get the ticket to contest the local municipal elections. He wanted to clean his image as a former gangster and was keen to be seen as a messiah of the masses. The constable left. This time, his mobile continued to ring.

Just then another man in need approached Altaf. Altaf asked him to pause and picked up the ringing mobile.

'Mr Altaf Sheikh?' he heard the honey-toned voice of a woman calling him by his first name. Altaf Sheikh brought the phone away from his ear to look at the display. No English-speaking lady had called him before. Moreover, no woman other than his mother had called him by his name. He was 'Sheikh Saab' for everyone. But he quite liked the sound of 'Mr Altaf Sheikh'.

'Hmm.' The gangster was terse. But that did not deter Monica. After all, he was her King of Swords. Her precious life depended on him.

'Altaf…Altaf…Altaf, I need you.'

Altaf looked at his phone yet again. Monica quickly corrected herself.

'I mean I need to meet you. You see, I am a photographer—'

'Photo-take-outer! Come, come!'

Altaf was excited. Some media coverage would definitely enhance his chances of contesting the elections.

7

*U*nlike her sprawling sea-facing houses on the posh hills of Bandra, Madanpura, in the heart of Central Mumbai, was an eye-opener. Literally. Her eyes were splayed open to avoid dashing the Bentley into people. There were so many of them! Some walked across despite moving traffic, overexcited schoolboys pushed one another, and zen-like goats meandered oblivious to the commotion. In sharp contrast to the oversized goats were the pint-sized spare parts workshops jostling for space. Bustling with street vendors selling mountains of food and clothes, the locality was dotted with mosques, dispensaries and shoddy, dilapidated two-storey stackhouses.

Many of the two-storey stackhouses looked like they were on the brink of collapse. Monica studied one such structure. It was teeming with life, its inhabitants blissfully unaware of the impending risk.

When 'Sheikh Manzil', a slightly better-constructed structure came into view, Monica pulled over. Madanpura froze in its tracks as everyone stopped their business and turned to stare at Monica as she got out of the car. Wearing oversized sunglasses, a fitted T-shirt and skinny jeans, with her smooth long hair fluttering behind her, she started to walk up Altaf's narrow wooden staircase. Towering pumps threw her off balance. Holding the railing, she climbed the rickety stairs. High-rise footwear was a bad idea after all.

From the road, she had not imagined how deep the structure would run, once inside. There was a multitude of tiny colourful rooms with open doors. Monica heard a blaring mix of sounds: a television news anchor from one room, a singer crooning on the radio from another, and the sound of a man pleading in the third.

'Water...water... I promise to start the water supply as soon as I get out of here. Please let me go!' Monica swallowed the lump that formed in her throat.

Just then, three burkha-clad women walked up the stairs lifting their veils. All three were stunning and stared openly at Monica. Knowing that she was out of place, Monica quickly said, 'Hi. I am here to meet Altaf.'

The ladies gasped at the blasphemy of hearing their Sheikh Saab's first name! The youngest of the three got defiant and stated, 'Sheikh Saab.'

Then the eldest of the three looked at the youngest, who drew the veil to cover her face yet again. As she took a step ahead, she signalled Monica to follow her through the winding wooden passage.

Moments later they stopped outside a door. The young wife entered and Monica followed suit.

Holding court, Altaf stopped when he saw his youngest wife sashay in. As a mark of respect, his cronies looked away to avoid meeting her eyes. Then Altaf saw Monica appear from behind his burkha-clad wife. He stared at her as she screamed, 'Altaf!'

A collective gasp. But that did not deter Monica. She continued, 'Altaf, I need to have a word with you in private.'

Altaf could not take his eyes off her. Bowled over by her beauty and sophistication, he flagged his hand off. The shocked bunch of people had to leave. Everyone obeyed, including his wife.

Once they were alone, Monica wasted no time.

'Altaf, I lied to you. Yes, I am a photographer, as in a photography student, but I have come to you for help. Please help me, Altaf.'

Dumbfounded, Altaf nodded. And for her part, for some inexplicable reason, Monica instantly felt safe in his presence. She began to recount her predicament. In English.

Altaf hung on to every word she spoke. There was an air of dignity about her. Suddenly his room was redolent with a melange of fragrances emanating from her hair and body. Moreover, the manner in which she spoke about her situation in fluent English clinched the deal for Altaf. He decided he would do everything in his capacity to save this damsel from the big bad world.

At the outset, Altaf let Monica speak without interrupting her. And that in itself was so therapeutic. At the end of her rant, she felt a tad lighter.

In broken English, Altaf told Monica that she was a 'very nice lady'. Next, he emphasized that he was not a gangster but a social worker who worked for the betterment of the people in his mohalla. Thirdly, he gave her his word, '*Sheikh ki zubaan.*'

Then he told her that she should not sully her image by getting gangsters...err...social workers involved in a family feud. Instead, she should go the legal way and speak to the police.

'No, Altaf. My father is a very influential man. He knows all the big guys,' pleaded Monica.

Altaf assuaged her anxiety by explaining that he had a very good friend in Bandra Police Station, Inspector Sunil Bhonsale. And the cop would certainly go out of the way for Monica at Altaf's behest. Bhonsale was an intelligent officer who would make sure that Monica was safe through the ordeal.

'*Zubaan, Sheikh ki zubaan*, Madam,' he assured Monica. Monica nodded and shrugged. What other choice did she have, after all?

Then Altaf called Inspector Sunil Bhonsale and told him that he was sending 'Madam Monica Singh' to him, and to give her 'full *corporation* in the *metter*'.

～

When Monica entered the buzzing Bandra Police Station, there was suddenly pin-drop silence. Everyone turned to stare at this glamorous diva. Aware of the effect she had created, Monica took a seat and twiddled her thumbs. Constables, complainants and detainees shuffled in their spots and looked at each other after striking furtive glances at the ravishing Monica. Junior officers spoke louder than usual and plaintiffs asserted their claims a tad forcefully. Both parties hoped to catch Monica's attention.

However, when thirty-two-year-old lanky and dark Sunil Bhonsale took his seat, the din in the police station fell silent yet again. This time it was due to fear of the no-nonsense police officer.

'Good afternoon, officer,' said Monica.

Sunil acknowledged her with a nod. A serious-looking Bhonsale then copiously took down all the details that Monica doled out.

'But Madam, why would they want to kill you? What is the motive?'

'I am not signing the papers.'

'So? They are angry, but that is no reason to kill.'

'I am ill at ease,' said Monica, mindful that the police inspector would not buy into the prophecy of the tarot.

'What do you mean you have not been feeling okay? What are your symptoms?'

'I can't explain it, officer, something in me just does not feel right. I have a weird feeling in the stomach, weakness and fatigue. Sometimes I feel I am coming down with a fever. But there is no fever.'

Sunil Bhonsale stared hard at Monica. After years of being a crime branch officer, he knew who was faking it. And Monica clearly wasn't.

Inspector Sunil Bhonsale summoned a lady constable.

'Surekha, take Madam for an urgent health check-up at the government hospital,' he ordered.

Monica resisted. 'Can I do the tests at a private clinic? I am not comfortable with government hospitals.'

'Madam, trust me, our hospitals are so well equipped that they have the antidote for every problem.'

When Monica tested positive for carrying the Marburg virus, Bhonsale picked a cigarette from his case and walked outside the precinct of Bandra Police Station. At first, he called the dean of the government hospital and requested her to take immediate action in Monica's case. Within five minutes, Monica was quarantined in an expansive room overlooking the sea. Next, antigens against Marburg were organized. Altaf was promptly informed.

Sunil Bhonsale thought it through as he lit a smoke: the

Marburg virus was unknown in India but could be traced to African countries. A study of Monica's passport showed that the last time she left the country was in June, that too for Madrid. She displayed all the early symptoms: weakness, fatigue and stomach ache. If left undiagnosed and untreated, Marburg could cause high fever, bleeding and shock. Finally, her organs would start to fail and she'd die because none of the private diagnostic centres would be able to test her for the elusive Marburg.

Taking a long drag, in his mind he ran through all the details of the incidents Monica had briefed him about.

Crushing the half-smoked cigarette under his heel, Inspector Sunil Bhonsale marched back to his office and snapped instructions to his constables in Marathi, '*Tya doctor la uthva rey!*' Then, gently slapping on the table his *girni patta*, the flour-mill belt infamously used in police interrogation, he stated slowly, 'I want Dr Sahay in my cabin by yesterday.'

⌒

In a dimly lit interrogation room which reeked of stale urine, Dr Sahay claimed that the injection he had given Monica contained lorazepam, a drug to ease panic attacks. But after getting gentle low-grade electric shocks on his testicles, the doctor confessed that the injections contained high doses of the Marburg virus, acquired by Abhay Suri from his friend's biotechnology company. The idea was that since there was no diagnosis or remedy for Marburg in India, Monica would succumb to it ultimately.

Sunil summoned the entire family to the police station. The four Suris were made to wait with commoners on a bench while Sunil Bhonsale took his time listening to a podcast in which filmmaker Francis Ford Coppola spoke about his challenges in making the cinematic masterpiece *The Godfather* in 1972.

The Suris were restless. Moreover, the heat intensified their distress. Ensconced in their air-conditioned life, they were unaware that the weather in Mumbai was this humid. But in police custody now, they could do nothing about the heat or the fact that they were being made to wait.

After an hour, Sunil called for them. The Suris noticed that there were no chairs opposite his wide table. As they stood, Sunil started slapping the girni patta on the table. While doing so he apprised them in a cold flat tone that he had enough evidence to press charges against Abhay Suri. And so, it was best if all of them left Monica alone. If she was harmed, maimed or killed, Abhay would be the first to get arrested, followed by the rest of the family for abetting the crime.

Papa Suri tried to intimidate Sunil by wielding the cliché, 'I know your boss. I can get you transferred from Bandra to Bhiwandi.'

'Should I make a call to the Enforcement Directorate?' asked Sunil coolly.

Papa Suri stammered in protest. Sunil raised his hand.

'Suri, you and your family are in my custody. You cannot leave this place unless you have my permission. I have enough evidence to arrest you all for abetting a murder. It is Friday today, and tomorrow the courts are shut. So, getting bail is out of the question. Unless you all want to spend the weekend in lock-up, please shut up.'

Papa Suri looked on as his ego shattered into tiny shards. Abhay and his mother were scared. Bhabhi Suri, on the other hand, was secretly impressed with Sunil Bhonsale. His power, his command over the language and, most importantly, his gumption were irresistible. Someone finally had the guts to talk back to the Suris.

After the Suris were dismissed, the next to be summoned to the station was To-Be-Ex-Husband Raghu Singh, who was dilly-dallying on the promises he had made.

Within an hour, inside a sea-facing duplex on Bandstand, Monica's favourite Manda was getting the house ready for her Madam.

The system of the law had put things in place.

Monica was overwhelmed by the benevolence of strangers when Altaf recounted all that had transpired in her absence. And she knew it was only possible because of Altaf. Here was an outsider, nothing like her ilk, but he cared for her more than her so-called family. Ever since he had received news of her quarantine, he checked on her well-being every hour. A tad amused by his genuine concern, her heart warmed to Altaf.

When Altaf saw a teddy bear graphic holding a thank you balloon from Monica on WhatsApp, he followed it up with an image of a princess sleeping under a get-well-soon duvet. That graduated to wishing each other flower-rich good mornings, sun-soaked happy afternoons and star-spangled good nights.

By the time she was discharged from the hospital and settled into her luxury apartment at Bandstand (nestled between Shah Rukh Khan's Mannat and Salman Khan's Galaxy Apartments), the graphic forwards got a notch respectful with Ramadan Kareem and Happy Iftar. And after Eid Mubarak, next in line were forwards about *friendship mein no sorry no thank you*, soulmates and karmic red threads.

When Altaf sent an image of the film poster of *Dil Chahta Hai*, Monica backed it up with that of *Kuch Kuch Hota Hai*. Altaf smiled and waited, for she was still online. Monica had never felt so playful. She then teased him with the poster of *Hum Aapke Hain Koun* followed by a question mark and he replied with the one of *Maine Pyar Kiya*. Corny, yes; cheesy—of course! But it was heartfelt.

৵

And while Monica was basking in the warmth of attention, back in Suri Manor, the parents refused to believe that Abhay could kill his sister. They despised Monica even more.

Now, safeguarding themselves against law enforcement was their agenda. Getting citizenship in a foreign country was not difficult. After all, banana republics like Honduras had always been welcoming to embezzlers of Indian banks. And the Suris were no different. However, they could not fly out.

'Let's drive into Nepal. I have fantastic connections there,' said Papa Suri. Abhay nodded and the ladies followed suit. But there were two things bothering his massive ego. First, how could his plan to poison Monica fail? Second, how dare she drag the family to the police?

Later that night, Abhay met Hitman. A contract killer. His job was to track Monica's movements and shoot her once Abhay and his family were out of the city.

8

After weeks of a restful eight hours of nightly sleep, coupled with noon naps and plenty of fresh fruit vegetable juices and hearty soups prepared under Manda's watchful gaze, Monica gained her health and vigour back. It was time to thank her King of Swords.

Now, parked under Altaf's chawl in Madanpura, Monica checked herself out in her car's sun visor mirror for the third time. She had always been crisp in her sartorial taste. And this was not a soirée where one had to look impeccable. Yet she was brushing her hair just two minutes after she had swept her fingers through it. She checked her teeth a third time over for anything that might be stuck in them. Was the blush too much? Maybe she should tone it down a shade, she thought.

Just then, two schoolgirls put their heads to the window and cupped the sides of their eyes to get a better view of this 'foreigner'. They simpered to each other with childish glee. That's when Monica put a stop to her unnecessary primping. She picked up her tote. Then, perching her cat-eye sunglasses on the bridge of her nose, she got out. The girls stared at this extraterrestrial beauty dressed in skinny denims teamed with a tailor-made white shirt. And no sky-scraping pumps like the last time. Everyone on the busy, claustrophobic square metre of plot stood in their tracks and froze their gazes on her. Monica looked at the girls and smiled tentatively. Suddenly shy, the girls recoiled in their respective tiny bodies and shut their eyes. Monica sashayed over to the entrance of Altaf's building and trekked up the steep stairs confidently. She was dressed for her King of Swords.

A hundred metres away, near the dilapidated two-storey stack-up, Abhay's Hitman surveyed the spot. A bustling street was perfect for murder, he thought.

When Monica walked to the room where they had first met, the doors were wide open. Inside, a police constable was seated with a box of *mithai* in his lap. There was also a wiry accomplice looking at the display of his mobile.

When the accomplice heard her shuffle in, he got up. Putting his hand on the chest, he bent slightly as a mark of respect. Then he informed Monica that his name was Ayan and 'Sheikh Saab' was working on an important matter. Ayan asked Monica to take a seat.

As she sat, the constable spoke to her.

'Sheikh Saab is a very good man, Madam. Our chawl had no water for days. Sheikh Saab made sure we get water twenty-four seven. Everybody is equal in the eyes of Sheikh Saab.'

Monica's spirit sank. Maybe she did not mean anything to Altaf after all. And now that the job was done, he had moved on. And that is how things were supposed to be.

Monica looked around the room knowing that she would never see him again. She got up to leave. And just then, Altaf stormed in followed by two cronies: a beefy Majid and a lanky Tahir.

'I thought I wasn't going to see you,' she looked adoringly into his eyes.

'Sorry, *agar pata hota ki tum aane wali ho toh nahi jaata*,' said Altaf. It was true. Altaf would not have left had he known she was coming to meet him. And then he added that he had gone to shut a country liquor bar in the mohalla and start a free library for poor children.

Impressed, Monica stared at him and he stared back at her. The chemistry between the sophisticated socialite and the crude gangster was palpable.

The constable butted in and thanked Sheikh Saab profusely. He promised that if Sheikh Saab ever stood for the elections, his chawl would vote for him. Saying this, he handed the box to Majid, who was standing behind the Sheikh, and left.

A beat of silence. Altaf slanted his head to the side. The henchmen were on guard now.

Altaf ordered them to wait outside for him, '*Humare aane tak bahar ruko. Kahi nahi jaana.*' Majid and Tahir started to vacate the room. The last to leave was Ayan.

Monica stared into Altaf's eyes till she heard the *click* of the shutting door. Both were alone in the room now. Monica could not contain herself and moved in closer. She hugged him.

'Thank you for saving my life, Altaf.'

Not expecting this display of affection, Altaf froze in his frame. He was not sure what the appropriate gesture was now.

Monica looked at him. Gingerly she touched one of his many scars and put her lips on it. Altaf slowly placed his palm on her back. His touch was electrifying and she looked up into his eyes. He stared back at her. And then slowly, very slowly, he put his lips on hers.

A quarter of an hour later, his three cronies, standing patiently outside the door, did not know how to react when they heard Altaf and Monica groan out loud. Majid, the beefy, well-worked-out henchman, pulled out a gun placed against the small of his back.

'What are you doing, Majid?' asked Ayan.

'That woman is trying to hurt Sheikh Saab!'

The other henchman, the lanky Tahir, started grinning and eventually burst out laughing. Ayan followed suit.

'*Kya?*' asked Majid. Tahir and Ayan laughed louder at Majid's question. He had no clue what was so funny.

'*Kabhie kiya nahi kya?*' Tahir asked whether Majid had never done 'it' and continued to laugh. Majid thought for a beat and then realized what was happening inside. He started to giggle too.

Just then Altaf's three wives sashayed in from the corridor, giggling at a private joke. The henchmen hushed up and hung their heads low, which was usual. They averted their gazes as a show of respect for Sheikh Saab's begums. Ayan rapped at the door to inform his boss. But Altaf was in the throes of ecstasy inside and could not be bothered. He was screaming in pleasure, unbridled, without a care in this world.

As his three begums walked past, at first they heard their Sheikh Saab moan and then Monica moan his name out loud. 'Altaf! Altaf! Altaf, yeah baby...ooh I love it, Altaf.' Then they heard both Altaf and Monica moan in unison, their decibels increasing a notch at a time.

The three wives stared at the henchmen. Not knowing how to react to the sounds of their husband fornicating with another woman right in their midst, they scurried away like building rats. Once they were out of sight, Majid looked at the group and said that they too should leave. Everyone agreed.

But then Tahir reminded them that Sheikh Saab had specifically mentioned that they wait till he came out. Now, not listening to Sheikh Saab would be blasphemy, would it not? And so, the cronies had no option but to stay put and hear Sheikh Saab and Monica fornicate in increasingly loud ecstasy.

∽

When the door finally opened, the day had turned to midnight. Altaf was the first to step out. He held Monica's hand gingerly. Both were spent, yet they were satiated. He escorted her down the rickety wooden steps to her car. Monica smiled as she got in.

'Bye baby,' she said, pecking his hand. He touched her chiselled face and she zoomed out in the darkest hour of the night.

As she drove, she was quiet. Looking up at the full moon and star-spangled sky, a sense of peace swathed her. Monica turned off the music. She wanted to soak in this peace that had evaded her for years now. The feeling of being desired lightened her spirit. Though she was sapped physically, her soul was renewed. There was no greater joy than knowing that one was safe, loved and desired. The world was suddenly a better place for Monica.

When she reached home, she did not want to bathe. She wanted to remember the evening, each moment. She had never had such a good time in bed. Her body was sore and she had that good ache in her limbs. Monica slipped out of her lingerie and was now naked under her duvet. She could not remember a single time she had been this wanton in bed.

Sex with To-Be-Ex-Husband was always sanitized. Sure, there was never any pain or soreness. But nor was there any joy or an orgasm. Moreover, it was always quick. Foreplay or post-coital nuzzling was a luxury he could not afford. But that was her dead past and she no longer wanted to carry it.

Reminiscing about the moments spent with Altaf, she fell into a deep slumber. A sleep so peaceful that it took away a lifetime of anguish.

9

To say that Mumbai traffic 'sucks' is an understatement. Bumper to bumper, elongated trails of vehicles, randomly dug roads, drivers honking impatiently, junctions choked by cars, the resulting air pollution and Mumbai's infamous clammy weather, which renders air conditioning redundant—road transportation within the city is a daylight horror. Moreover, the upcoming underground metro has given rise to motorway blocks that roast commuters, physically as well as psychologically.

But Monica was undeterred in the face of it all. And from the next day, day after day, every day, she braved peak-hour slow-moving traffic and drove from Bandstand to Madanpura only to satiate her carnal needs.

Post coitus, one afternoon, Monica and Altaf caught their breaths. Altaf had a drink of water from the fridge and, offering the bottle to Monica, asked her what she would like to eat.

'What? No, nothing at all. I am good,' she said.

'What no every day? After so much hard work, not hungry? Good food in Madanpura. *Yaha ki nalli nihari khaogi toh duniya bhool jaogi.* You will forget the world if you have Madanpura's nalli nihari.'

'It's fine, Altaf, I am on keto.'

'*Array yaar toh keto kaun si badi baat hain!* What's the big deal about keto?'

'You know what the keto diet is?'

'Madam, rich, poor, high class, low class, all loves three things.'

'What are those three things, Altaf?'

'Love, food, *aur* diet *ki baaten.*'

Monica chuckled at his earthiness. And the truth was endearing. Food and conversations about diet and weight loss have always been great equalizers.

'*Madanpura ke kebab khaogi toh duniya bhool jaogi.*' Repeating this, he called Ayan and asked for '*ek mutton biryani, ek plate seekh kebab, aur ek plate murgh tikka.*'

'That is a lot of food, Altaf!'

Altaf beamed at what he thought was a compliment. He was the king of this fiefdom and would eat like one with his lady love.

Twenty minutes later, as Monica walked down the corridor to another room, she asked Altaf, 'Who lives in these rooms? They seem to be empty.'

Altaf mentioned that he owned the place and opened the door for her. Monica entered. Ayan had laid out a spread of just-hot-off-the-coal kebabs, mutton biryani, and Altaf's much-loved thick and spicy nalli nihari. Taking a seat, she smiled. When Altaf sat next to her, on cue Ayan walked out, shutting the door behind him.

Altaf picked up the plate of seekh kebabs and started to serve her extra-large portions of meat.

'Altaf stop, that's too much food!'

Next, with his hand, he tore a piece of grilled seekh from her plate and fed it to her. The spices tingled, tickling her taste buds, and she enjoyed every bite. Next, she tore a small bite of naan from his plate and dipped it in the spice-laden gravy of nalli nihari. She put it near his mouth. Altaf smiled and took a bite.

And while he fed her large helpings of keto-approved grills with his hands, Monica remembered those petite portions she gingerly helped herself to under To-Be-Ex-Husband's watchful gaze. In fact, that was standard practice amongst all her so-called friends. They ate petite portions in front of their husbands and binged on biryani later. Soon after, it would be purged from their systems for the fear of becoming fat. In her former world, 'fat' was the worst thing that a wife could be.

'Altaf! Stop. I will get fat.' She giggled, then followed up her complaint by gorging on a chunk of pahari kebab dipped in feisty green pudina chutney. The flavours of heaven were in her mouth.

'But what is wrong with fat?' asked Altaf in a strenuous attempt at English. A wry smile flitted across Monica's stuffed face as Altaf sucked on his nalli and then sucked a mouthful of gravy. Nothing mattered in that moment, not even Altaf chomping on his food noisily.

Until her sex fete with Altaf, Monica was unaware of the sexual beast that lay dormant within her being. Very often Monica tried to match Altaf's brutal energy and, in the process, hurt him with her acrylic talons. And by the end, Altaf's body was riddled with sharp nail marks. Once, in the heat of lust, her nails ripped through his body with such fervour that Altaf yelped in agony.

The next day, Monica went to a nail spa and chipped off her colourful, sparkling fake nails. Looking at her short and bare unpolished stubs now, she felt...well, naked. She couldn't remember the last time she had lived with her real nails. Involuntarily, she brought her digits to her face and kissed them.

The nail attendant thought she had lost the plot, but Monica realized that she had stopped caring what people thought of her. Just then, the truth sunk in... She was changing, becoming more of who she was truly meant to be. She was eating a few carbs now and found that she was not as anxious as she used to be. Moreover, she was eating well, not binging and later purging her much-loved biryani. She would bite into a well-cooked tender piece of mutton on a bed of saffron rice and enjoy each morsel in the company of a man who was crazy about her.

And after her meal, they would walk around the mohalla. That's one thing Altaf and Monica did when they were not making love or eating.

Guarded by henchmen, the couple took walks around the neighbourhood, unaware that they were being trailed by Hitman.

Altaf wanted to flaunt his glamorous English-speaking 'girlfriend'. And the strolls thrilled Monica just as much. The sights and sounds of a world frozen in time whetted the amateur photographer in her. She noticed the beauty of the graceful old-world architectural style of the beams despite the cracks and blackish-grey mould they were covered in. She had never experienced this world first-hand; her only reference was Bollywood films. On seeing a run-down chawl inside a dark alley, Monica exclaimed, 'Oh my God, this is so *Satya!*' When she clicked an old toothless vendor with a skull cap running with a stick after eight-year-olds playing gully cricket, she mused, 'I feel as if I am in the Wasseypur village.' The more she announced her enchantment, the more it pleased Altaf.

Monica pointed to the dilapidated structure that had always worried her. 'Altaf, look at the building. It could come crashing down at any moment. There are families living inside. You need to protect them.'

Altaf wanted to impress her. Besides, looking after the welfare of people in the mohalla would earn him brownie points.

Within a week, the structure was emptied of its residents. Altaf had organized temporary accommodation for them in a transit camp close by. The municipal corporation was notified and the usual cycle of red tape commenced on which builder to give the redevelopment scheme to.

And one day, Hitman got three missed calls from a classified number. He knew it was time to obliterate the target.

⌒

The following afternoon, while composing a frame of an old art deco building discovered bang in the heart of the mohalla, Monica's phone rang. She ignored her ringing mobile as she aimed for a shot.

Unknown to her, a few metres away, hiding inside the dilapidated structure emptied by Altaf a week ago, Hitman aimed his gun at Monica's temple. And just as he was about to pull the trigger, the tottering structure started to shake. Moments later its walls and ceilings came down like an avalanche, crushing his skull. The hitman died on the spot! His body was hidden under the rubble.

Monica, Altaf and his henchmen, and then the entire mohalla gathered to witness the structure crumble to the ground. Everyone praised Sheikh Saab's foresight and how he had saved families, yet again. Altaf looked into Monica's eyes. He was grateful for her warning. They smiled at each other. All was well in this pocket of the universe.

But that was not the case for the Suris. They had planned to escape from India via Nepal. However, they could not go beyond Mumbai as they were stopped by the traffic police at Panvel. There was a red alert about the Suris planning an escape.

Back in the Suri Manor now, Abhay tried to call Hitman but could not get through. He was frustrated.

Just as Raghu was frustrated at the moment. In his swanky office, Luckshmi gave him the shocking news. Nine out of his core team of ten had been poached by his rivals. Raghu was stumped! His core team had been with him for almost twenty years. They were as good as family. This unfortunate turn of events just did not make sense. How was it even possible?

10

Monica was back to shooting the decrepit art deco building after the interruption of the collapse of the tottering structure the previous day. Altaf looked at her with pride as she adjusted the height of the tripod.

Now her phone rang. At first, she ignored it. But the persistent ringing was disturbing her focus, so she reached out for her phone in order to put it on silent mode. But when she looked at the display, she immediately answered the caller. It was Hormuzd Cawasji.

'Sir! Hello.'

'I don't have time for students who bunk class and are disinterested. I want to make place for someone who really wants to learn. Tara is out and the next one is you. Don't come from tomorrow.'

'Sir, sir...no... No... Please don't do that.'

Altaf frowned as he took a step toward her. Monica stepped away from him.

'I can explain, sir. I was in a lot of trouble.'

'Were you dying?'

'Kind of, sir.'

'Don't bullshit me. Anyway, don't come to class. I want a deserving student. There are plenty on the wait list.'

'Sir, please try to understand—'

'You know, Monica, I was so impressed when you signed up for the photography contest, even though I knew you were not ready. Gifted, yes, but not yet ready. You simply wasted your time and mine.'

Saying this, Cawasji hung up. Crestfallen, Monica stared at the display of her mobile.

Altaf rolled up his sleeves and asked who it was on the other end of the line. '*Kaun tha…*'

'Stop it, Altaf. He is my teacher. He means well.'

'*Phir mooh kyon latkaya hai?*' Altaf could not understand why Monica looked so glum if the call was by her well-meaning teacher.

'You know, Altaf, for the first time in my life someone called me gifted. Someone saw promise, a talent in me. Someone said I had something special to offer. And I let that person down.'

'*Tum special ho, Monica.*'

Monica did not react. She was staring at her camera. After a beat, she said, 'Altaf! Please show me places no one has ever seen before.'

Altaf beamed.

Minutes later he walked her through a maze of mean streets. Altaf claimed that without permission, no crime reporter or police officer had access to this patch of the city.

Monica thought she was in a dream as she treaded through the gossamer of drifters, squalor, decrepit old-world homes, and prostitutes with their oiled hair tied into double plaits, wearing garish make-up.

'Gafoor Santra here, my man shot,' said Altaf pointing to an open gutter.

Monica raised her camera to take a picture of a prostitute

seated on her haunches cooking chicken curry on a wood fire right next to it. Her toddlers were running around, avoiding the gutter deftly.

'What kind of a surname is Santra?' asked Monica when she started to click.

Altaf then explained that it was his mafia code name. Gafoor was a wholesale fruit merchant and so they referred to him as Santra, 'orange' in Hindi.

'Faheem Mach-Mach shot there,' said Altaf, pointing to a narrow space between two rundown structures. An old typist had set his business in there—a table, a chair, a typewriter and a tattered canopy that covered him from the sun and bird shit.

Monica nodded as she looked into the viewfinder and muttered, 'Which means this Faheem guy spoke too much, is it?' Saying this, she froze the old typist in her frame.

Altaf was impressed and wondered how she guessed it. '*Array wah! Tumhe kaisey pata?*'

Monica looked at Altaf and blew a kiss.

That night Monica carefully studied the pictures she had taken. Then she curated five images of the sights of Madanpura and sent them to Hormuzd Cawasji.

The teacher was having his tipple of beer when his WhatsApp started to sound off at alarming speed. An ardent fan of photography, Cawasji studied the pictures. They were so real and well-timed that they impressed the hard-to-please-but-well-meaning photography teacher.

He texted her, 'Welcome back.' When she reported the same to Altaf, he beamed. He decided he'd show her around some more...

ﮛ

From his sources, Abhay Suri found out that all was bright and beautiful with Monica. However, Hitman had disappeared without a trace. They also informed him that she was seen with an ex-gangster. Abhay was on his guard. Had the gangster made Hitman disappear? Abhay realized that he needed to get Monica when she was not with the gangster. When she was out of Madanpura, that is...

And yet again, his evil mind started to think...

ﮛ

After a hectic stint of street photography, Monica and Altaf were walking towards his Sheikh Manzil. It was twilight and the entire chawl was lit up with shimmering tea lights.

'Getting married for the fourth time, Altaf?' asked Monica, poking him playfully.

Altaf blushed and explained that his daughter Ilham had got 'first class' in the first-term exams. When Monica enquired about the percentage scored, she found that it was 60.5 per cent, enough to make Altaf happy and for his wives to prepare mutton khichada for all. As they came closer to home, Monica saw one of Altaf's five sons cleaning the windows of her car with a mop.

'Why is your son cleaning *my* car?'

'Only 45 per cent,' said Altaf, looking at him as he flared his nostrils in anger. And then he pointed to the other two. They were cleaning two-wheelers.

Monica looked at them and asked, 'Less than 45 per cent.'

Tch! A disappointed Altaf nodded his head.

'But Altaf, you barely studied till the seventh grade. At least the boys have cleared their exams.'

Altaf looked into Monica's eyes. '*Mujhe apne jaisa nahi banana hai inn bachchon ko,*' he confessed. He didn't want the kind of life he had led for his children, and only a solid education would help them change their world. He wanted the best for them, like any other parent.

Monica wished she could capture his vulnerability in a frame. But that would be insensitive at the moment.

ᴖᴖ

Altaf opened the doors to his personal world for Monica. He introduced her to his sons, his studious pre-teen daughter Ilham and his three gorgeous wives: Khatijeh, Baareeka and Asharfi. Monica could not be sure whether they genuinely did not mind her presence or whether the wives were hiding their acrimony for fear of backlash from Altaf.

Monica clicked pictures of them with gusto: Altaf preparing tea for his daughter Ilham as she studied for her seventh standard Olympiad; laughing with Ilham's mother Khatijeh, his eldest wife, while she showed him something on the phone. Next, him helping plump Baareeka and her sons lift the sofa so that she could make space for the recently purchased stationary cycle. The family needed to exercise, he explained. Then without his knowledge, Monica clicked him as he stood by the window and slanted a stern glance at the twenty-seven-year-old Asharfi. She was on the balcony watching virile young men her age play gully cricket in the mohalla.

Suddenly, there was an uproar. It was so loud that Altaf, followed by Monica, Khatijeh, Baareeka and three of the boys rushed to the balcony. All of them looked over each other's shoulders to see the source of the ruckus. As the pandemonium grew, Ilham left her studies and joined the huddle on the balcony.

'*Array*, that Hidaaya and Reham are at it again,' concluded Khatijeh as she nodded her head. Then, turning around, she planted her palm on Ilham, and the mother–daughter duo ambled into the house. The rest of the family followed suit, leaving Altaf and Monica alone on the balcony.

'Nothing new,' Altaf smirked.

But it was very amusing for Monica to watch two drop-dead gorgeous women, in hijab and abaya, hurl the choicest abuses at each other. One seemed to be in her early forties and the other looked like she was edging towards her fifties.

The phrases they used were colourful, with such graphic descriptions as '*Main ghasargundi se aakar tere dhunggan main sandal ghusaongi!*' As the two ladies raved at each other about whizzing down a slide to shove their sandals up the other's buttocks, Monica propped up her camera and zoomed into the fight, while Altaf explained the cause of the fury.

The younger of the duo, Reham, was forty. The elder one, her neighbour Hidaaya, was only forty-five. Reham was married off to Al-Noor when she was around eighteen, her husband being forty back then. She was his fourth wife. Now Al-Noor was in his sixties, dabbling in dentures and diabetes. And Hidaaya's twenty-seven-year-old virile son Afaan and Reham, who was at the peak of her sexuality, were madly in love.

Monica looked up from the viewfinder and stared at Altaf. He told her not to look so shocked as this was a common cause of skirmish in his mohalla. As Monica returned to framing her shots, she asked Altaf, 'So if this happens twenty years later with Asharfi, you won't be so surprised, is it?'

Altaf stared hard at the trigger-happy Monica. When she looked back at him, the two burst into peals of laughter.

⌀

The next day, Monica showed Hormuzd Cawasji the pictures she had taken in Altaf's home as well as those of Madanpura. Cawasji was impressed by her composition and timing.

'You must keep practising, Monica. That is the only way to success.'

'Sir, are any of these any good to send for the contest?'

'Um, let's see.'

Saying this, Cawasji leaned into the screen of her laptop to study the images.

⌀

'Are you kidding me?! He actually told you that he has shot gangsters called Santra and Mach-Mach?' gushed Tara as she took a sip of her vodka. They were sitting in Monica's palatial home with a view of the Arabian Sea. Monica took a sip of her crisp white wine and nodded.

'But doesn't it scare you to be with someone like that?'

'My brother tried to kill me. My husband betrayed me. No one judges them. Why should I judge Altaf? Anyway, tell me what's up with you, Tara,' asked Monica, curling her legs comfortably on the sofa.

'I am going to Canada next month.'

'Wow, with Dhruv? That's exciting!'

'I know, but I also do know it isn't going to last.'

'Don't be such a pessimist.'

'It is not me; it is my tarot. You know now that it doesn't lie.'

Monica shrugged. She could not refute that.

Tara turned to Monica. 'So tell me. Are you in love with Altaf?'

'No. I am just attracted to him. His life is so different from mine... I see everything through a fresh prism.'

'What about him?'

'Tara, I think we are both old enough to know that there can be a relationship without expectations.'

'That's what you think, Monica. Does he think the same way?'

Monica did not have an answer. Tara added, 'Does he love you?' Monica looked at Tara, who continued, 'Because if he loves you, and you don't, then that's wrong. You are leading him on.'

Monica paused and then took a slow sip as the gravity of Tara's words sunk in.

11

*M*onica did not know how to broach the topic with Altaf. She was unsure how he would react. So instead of informing him head-on, she decided she'd wean him off her. From driving to Madanpura every day, Monica at first started to visit him thrice a week. Calculating two weeks hence, she dropped it to twice a week.

As time passed, she realized that Altaf's WhatsApp forwards now seemed garish for her refined taste. His chomping loudly on nalli nihari now started to bother her.

'Stop it! Too much noise,' she snapped one afternoon.

'*Tumhe kya ho gaya?*' asked Altaf as he slurped a large sip of gravy wondering what happened to make her so irritable.

'I have been eating too much food. I need a break,' said Monica. There was an awkward pocket of silence. 'And... yes. I forgot to tell you; I need to edit my pictures with my photography professor.' Saying this, Monica shrugged as Altaf stared at her.

Monica wasn't exactly lying, because she had now surrendered herself to her hobby. Honing her skills as a shutterbug was her top priority. Instead of Madanpura, she now fancied the last of the existing cottages and bungalows of Bandra.

When Monica did not return Altaf's calls or texts for a week, he started getting suspicious. So he took Majid's cell phone to call her. Luckily, Monica was with Hormuzd Cawasji at the time who was teaching her how to edit, and the phone was on silent mode. Altaf was relieved.

Monica was so engrossed in editing that even when she saw a missed call on her phone, she did not bother to call back. However, when she saw that Tara had sent her a WhatsApp text, she started typing her reply. Just then, Altaf called her on WhatsApp asking for an explanation for being missing in action. He demanded to see her the following day.

'No, Altaf, I am exhausted and I have a really bad headache. I will call you when I feel better.' Saying this, she hung up.

When Altaf did not hear from her days later, he once again stalked her on WhatsApp. The moment she was online, he dialled her number.

'I was just about to call you, Altaf. I have been super busy helping Tara pack for Canada,' said Monica. In her palatial apartment, she sipped on orange juice while looking at stills of Madanpura on her Mac. Altaf insisted on seeing her the following day.

'Sorry, baby, I have to drop Tara off at the airport tomorrow.'

'*Aye!* Who you think you are, *rey*?! Don't phorget I am gangster!' Altaf roared.

'But you said you were a social worker,' said Monica.

Altaf paused.

Monica hung up on him and blocked his number. She was done with Altaf Sheikh. Putting the phone away, she colour-corrected the image of Altaf staring angrily at Asharfi. Without emotion, she glanced keenly at the screen while culling out the perfect image. Photography was now her calling.

∽

Back in Suri Manor, Abhay was studying the fake passports made for the four of them. The plan was to escape the country via the Arabian Sea route. He had to coordinate with officers he could bribe at Mazagaon docks.

Abhay's sources informed him that Monica was no longer going to Madanpura, but was seen mostly around the villages of Bandra. This time, Abhay called Truckman. His job was to run his truck into Monica and make it look like an accident.

∽

Days later, Monica woke up while it was still dark outside. She hopped out of bed and changed from her vests and shorts into comfortable track pants, a T-shirt and shoes. As she rummaged around for her keys, mobile and wallet, she noticed that the sky was turning from black to deep purple. Putting her belongings into her camera bag, she headed out the door. She wanted to click the towering steeples of Mount Mary Church in the nick of time, just as the morning rays illuminated them. Usually, she would have walked to the church as it was close to home. A morning walk uphill would have done her good. However, since she had to wait till daybreak, Monica decided to take her car.

She drove and parked outside the precincts of the church at a point where she had a clear view of its soaring steeples. Monica got out with her camera and leaned against her car. Just then, she felt cold metal touch the small of her back. When Tahir and Majid came into view, she realized the cold metal was the muzzle of a pistol.

Both men were armed with pistols. Majid asked her to sit in the car. As she took the driver's seat, he sat next to her. Tahir went to the back seat. Majid folded his hands in such a way that the muzzle of the pistol was surreptitiously pointing at her arm. Tahir also pointed his gun in her direction. They asked her to drive. Monica felt a lump in her throat as she drove to Madanpura that morning.

Altaf was pacing the room. Majid walked in, followed by Monica, with Tahir tailing her. Altaf stared at Monica and then looked at his henchmen. On cue, Majid and Tahir left the room.

Altaf knew why Monica was turning his back on him. '*Mujhe pata hai tum mujhse bhaag kyon rahi ho... Yehi na ki main shaadi-shuda hoon aur tum meri girlfriend?*'

'Altaf, it has nothing to do with you being married, and I am not your girlfriend—'

Altaf lifted his palm to make her pause mid-sentence. He knew better after all. That is why he had sent for her. '*Sab jaanta hoon. Isi liye toh tumhe yahaan laya hoon.*'

Monica stared hard at Altaf. 'You did not send for me, Altaf. You had me kidnapped. Moreover, I drove the car in my own kidnapping.'

Altaf went down on his knees. He wanted her to be his wife. His intentions were noble—he wanted marriage, after all. '*Begum bano meri. Main tumse nikah karna chahta hoon.*'

'Altaf, are you out of your mind?'

Indeed he was. Love was madness, after all. '*Hai yeh ishq, yeh pagalpann nahi toh aur kya hai?*'

Monica was shocked. She finally blurted, 'Altaf, I don't love you.'

Now it was Altaf's turn to be shocked. What the hell was she doing with him for all those months then? '*Toh itne mahine se mere saath kya kar rahi ho!*'

Monica paused for a beat to figure out the right things to say. 'Look, I like you, and you are great fun to be with—'

Fun? Was he just a way to pass time for her? '*Toh main tumhara time pass tha?*'

Monica paused. She did not know what to say.

Altaf was stunned, his ego crushed. Then he started insisting that they get married that very day. '*Nikah, main tumse nikah karoonga. Aaj hi.*'

'Altaf, don't be stupid.'

Altaf thought Monica was reluctant because he already had three wives. So he promised her three things: that she would be his favourite wife, that he would sleep in her bedroom every night, and that she would not need to wear a burkha like the rest. '*Tum meri sabsey favourite begum rahogi. Aur harr raat main tumharey paas rahunga. Aur tumhe burkha pehenney ki zarurat nahi.*'

Monica burst into tears. 'Don't do this, Altaf. I don't want to marry you.'

Altaf's heart melted when he saw her cry. He hugged her. After all, everyone got cold feet at the mention of marriage. Eventually they get used to it. '*Array pagli, shaadi ka darr sabhi ko lagta hai. Dheere dheere aadat pad jayegi.*'

Monica stopped crying as she stared at him. Was he delusional?

Just then there was a brief knock on the door, and Khatijeh walked in with a tray laden with breakfast: bread, keema and boiled eggs. She was followed by Baareeka, who carried a tray filled with teacups and a kettle.

When Asharfi walked in, Altaf growled, 'Where are you going so early in the morning?' For her body was completely swathed in her burkha, exposing just the slits of her sharp twinkling eyes. Asharfi mentioned that they had heard he was getting married to Monica, so they would need to buy some jewellery and other knick-knacks for the wedding. Saying this, she asked Altaf for money.

As Altaf dug into his pockets for currency notes, Baareeka handed Monica a cup of tea. Khatijeh started putting food on the plate. Next, Baareeka handed Altaf his tea. Monica could not bring herself to have a drink. She was petrified.

Altaf sat at the table and slurped loudly from the cup. As he glugged down his tea, Monica stared at him. In that moment, she could not believe that she had been attracted to him at one time. Subsequently, Khatijeh put his plate of keema pav and boiled eggs on the table and told Altaf that he could not see Monica till the marriage was solemnized.

Altaf continued to bite into his breakfast while the four women walked away. Tahir and Majid stood in the passage. They looked away, avoiding gazing at the women. Asharfi turned around and asked Monica to hand over the car keys to her as she had to go shopping. Quietly, Monica dipped her hands into her pockets and handed the keys to Asharfi. The four ladies entered the family flat and shut the door on Tahir and Majid.

Minutes later, when the door opened and they saw the folds of a black gown, Majid and Tahir looked away. Asharfi then sashayed down and, pressing the button to unlock Monica's car, got in and drove out of the henchmen's sight.

The burkha-clad lady in the car was Monica. Altaf's wives had plotted her feeble escape after getting to know that Monica was least interested in him.

Now, as the car reached the flyover, Monica pulled the mouth scarf down and took a deep breath. The drama that had ensued since morning sunk in, and she heaved.

Just then a car ranged into view and kept pace with her. Monica slid a glance at it and was shocked to see Tahir and Majid in a Wagon R trying to push her car to the side. Monica pressed her sneaker on the accelerator and a chase ensued from JJ flyover all the way to Bandra.

As she entered Hill Road, she did not know what to do as the car followed her steadily. It was a matter of time before they'd catch up with her and kidnap her again. Her spirit continued to plummet down a dark abyss, until…wait… hang on…it saw a ray of light! A hundred metres ahead of her was Bandra Police Station on the opposite side! And who could it be but Inspector Sunil Bhonsale stepping out for smoke!

Monica pressed her foot on the accelerator and her thumb on the horn, creating a ruckus. Just then, a speeding truck came roaring towards her car. In the nick of time, Monica took a U-turn and drove towards Bhonsale.

The truck drove past with speed. Tahir, who was driving, froze in his seat when he saw the truck careening towards him. Truckman lost control. Tahir and Majid flew out of their seats right before the truck crashed into the Wagon R, smashing it flat against a building compound. Thanking their lucky stars, Tahir and Majid fled the scene as quickly as they could. Meanwhile, the truck driver was gheraoed by passers-by and was beaten up.

A commotion ensued.

Bhonsale looked at the car moving menacingly towards him and removed a gun from his holster. Just then, the speeding car came to an abrupt halt. Getting out, Monica ran towards Inspector Sunil Bhonsale.

'Inspector, please, please help me. Altaf's men are trying to kidnap me.'

'Who? Whose men?'

'Altaf. Sheikh... Sheikh Saab.'

Sunil paused to stare at Monica. Her sincere eyes were pleading for protection.

'Get inside,' he ordered and called for his constables. Making sure that Monica had a lady constable attending to her, Bhonsale buckled down to work. Monica watched him as he called the control room and informed them about two armed young men who had abandoned a silver Wagon R that was now flattened in a truck accident. He asked for an SOS *nakabandi* across the exits as well. Next, he rushed out hastily and got into a police car that zipped away.

Surekha, the lady constable, got Monica a glass of water. Monica held her arm as she mumbled a quick thank-you and glugged it down to its last dregs. Then a duty officer got a thick file, and opening it, he started to question Monica. Just as she was about to tell him what had transpired, she heard a commotion. Monica turned around to see Tahir and Majid fall to the floor begging for mercy. Standing at the threshold, Sunil Bhonsale glowered at the two.

'We did not do anything, sir.'

'We are innocent, sir.'

Monica had never seen Majid quiver like a chicken picked for a chop. Bhonsale ordered the two to be locked up. While they were getting dragged away, Majid saw Monica and begged, '*Shishter! Behen, ghar ka mamla hai.*'

Sunil slapped Majid hard across his face. 'Forget speaking

to her. Don't you dare even look at her!' Saying this, he repeated the stinging assault. The men were dragged into lock-up. While Monica could not see them, she could hear the sound of a whip and a yelp. Whip and yelp, whip and yelp, like a rhythmic tune. Then Sunil Bhonsale stormed out to where Monica sat and asked the duty officer to make a detailed written complaint. In that moment, there was something about Sunil that struck terror in the most fearless of hearts. Despite him being on her side, she too was petrified of the police officer's ire.

Sunil held his phone and, dialling a number, walked out. By the time he found an empty spot in the backyard of the police station, Altaf answered the phone. Sunil knew he had to be very tactful with this associate.

As they spoke, Altaf's cronies were beaten to a pulp in police lock-up.

Sunil informed Altaf about the turn of events. That Monica was under his aegis as she had complained about being kidnapped. To which Altaf replied that he had no intentions of kidnapping her but wanted to marry her.

'But Monica Singh clearly does not want to marry you.'

Altaf paused to listen as Sunil Bhonsale slowly explained to Altaf that if he filed a complaint, it would be a case of kidnapping. And when it came to kidnapping and rape, the law was stringent and his seniors would get involved. 'I will not be able to do anything, Sheikh.'

Altaf asked Sunil how he could save himself.

'Just stay away from Monica Singh. Simple.'

Altaf agreed readily and thanked Sunil for his foresight. Next, Sunil asked Altaf what had to be done about his boys. Altaf suggested that they should remain in lock-up for a couple of days. That would teach them a lesson for not taking care of his brand-new Wagon R.

Then Sunil walked back to his cabin and sat opposite Monica. 'Madam, you can go home now.'

'What?! No, no way. I am not going home. Altaf will find my whereabouts… I am scared to go home.'

'Madam, I promise you, there will be no repercussions.'

'I trust you, officer, but I don't trust Altaf. If he changes his mind, he will know where to find me. And I can't go back to my family.'

'Do you have any friends?'

'Tara…but she is in Canada.'

'You could check into a five-star hotel, Madam.'

'Still…I won't be safe there,' Monica looked away helplessly and paused to think. And then, after a moment, she stared reflectively at Sunil. 'If there is anyone in the city I am safe with, it is you, officer.'

Though he was taken aback, Sunil remained poker-faced. He was one of those whose face revealed nothing.

'I am really scared. And you are the only one I trust. I won't cause any trouble to you or your family.'

'I don't have one in Mumbai,' said Sunil.

12

Her car halted yet again. It was a Monday evening in Mumbai and one could not spot an empty patch of asphalt on roadways across the city. Snaking trails of automobiles inched bit by bit, painfully making their way to their chosen destinations. Until a few years ago, south-bound traffic was manageable at twilight, but of late it did not matter where one was going. Furthermore, the ongoing construction of the underground metro had narrowed the navigable space, making the situation worse. Regardless of the time of day or mode of transport, hapless commuters had to crawl their way to any part of the city.

While most looked at their phones involuntarily, an excited Monica asked questions in her car. Seated next to her, Inspector Sunil Bhonsale's answers were swift and to the point.

'Sir, where are you from?'

'Pune, Madam.'

'Oh okay...so is that where you were born?'

'And studied, yes.'

'And your wife? She lives there now?' Monica asked tentatively as she put her car in first gear and moved ahead slowly. Sunil looked at her.

'I am not trying to get personal, officer... I just don't want to create a problem, you see. I have been married in the past, so I respect that space. And ours is a very unusual situation here,' Monica rambled, over-explaining herself while she gently put her sneaker over the brake.

'That won't be necessary, Madam. I have been a divorcee for five years now.'

'Oh!' piped Monica. She had not seen it coming. 'Divorcee'—the tag chafed her nerves. Grappling for words, she shrugged. And then, asked something very typical, although unnecessary. 'Any plans to remarry?'

Sunil looked at her, his face deadpan as usual. 'Excuse me for the language, Madam.' Monica turned to Inspector Sunil Bhonsale. He looked away and stared at the boot of the car in front of them. 'My ex-wife was Bengali. Every time we fought, she'd call me *bokachoda*. "Bokachoda" means "dumb-fuck".'

Monica paused to stare as Sunil Bhonsale continued, 'I am not one, I know. *Par agar main dobara vohi galati karunga, toh bokachoda hi banunga na?* But if I repeat the same mistake, it indeed makes me a bokachoda, does it not?'

Unsure of whether to react or not, Monica moved the gear from neutral to first. The car inched ahead as the weight of Bhonsale's words sunk in.

There was a lull. Then, Bhonsale informed Monica that he lived in a simple middle-class Maharashtrian housing colony. If he walked in with a burkha-clad woman, it would create unnecessary gossip.

'So, you do care what people think of you, officer?'

'Madam, my job is to melt into the milieu and not stand out.'

Monica smiled. As soon as her car slowed to a halt at

the signal, with great speed and dexterity she got out of her burkha. One by one, she handed the headscarf and the gown to Sunil, who looked on tentatively as he touched the black fabric. It had been a long time since he had touched a woman's clothes. Then, folding it neatly, he placed it on the back seat next to her camera. Meanwhile, the signal turned green and Monica swerved to the left. Minutes later, she drove into Samruddhi Co-operative Housing Society.

Located in the heart of Dadar, the colony was built at a time when space in the island city was freely available. Now, Monica's car glided into a sprawling estate and parked itself gracefully without a fight, which is unusual anywhere else in Mumbai. Getting out, she looked around. It was a rectangular expanse of land bordered by five-storey buildings starting from Block A all the way to Block E. As she looked around, Sunil informed her that, built in 1946, this was one of the first cooperative housing societies in Mumbai.

From where she walked, the entire colony looked like a mosaic of tiny rectangles coloured randomly with yellow or blue lights. Some rectangles were black as the lights in those flats were out. Women cooked inside a column of windows, an old man looked out the balcony, one fellow smoked away, a woman bobbed her newborn infant, another filled his glass with a peg of Old Monk, and children ran around playing their evening games.

'So many lives, so many destinies, playing out in a single piece of land,' said Monica as she entered B-Block.

She noticed there was no lift.

As he walked up, Sunil added, 'The great mystery that we call destiny plays out in just a thousand square feet of land, flat by flat.'

Monica smiled. She was impressed. Sunil stopped at the first door on the first floor. His name was etched in bold on the nameplate: Sunil Sakharam Bhonsale. He twirled the key and opening the door to his flat, said, 'Welcome, Madam.'

Monica stepped in and looked around. And the first thing she noticed was books! Thirty-year-old Sunil's functional home was pulsating with gems of pure crime thrillers. Contemporary page-turners of Stephen King, David Baldacci, James Patterson, Lee Child, Jo Nesbo, Stieg Larsson, Don Winslow and Steve Hamilton stuck to each other like a thick group of high-school buddies. Taut works of James M. Cain, Raymond Chandler and James Hadley Chase were stacked on the top shelf, almost like gods on an altar. But what charmed Monica was a slew of women authors who took centre stage in a nook crammed with noir—Gillian Flynn, Paula Hawkins, Megan Miranda and, much to her surprise, Daphne Du Maurier's *Rebecca*. Then there were the book versions of Quentin Tarantino's screenplays—*Pulp Fiction*, *True Romance* and *Reservoir Dogs*. There were hardbacks on film craft focusing on writing and cinematography; some Wong Kar-wai DVDs like *Chungking Express* and *Happy Together*, along with a box set of Alfred Hitchcock masterpieces. She also noticed the biographies of two filmmakers who struck gold in the 1970s—Martin Scorsese and Francis Ford Coppola.

Right away, Monica was comfortable in Sunil's cluttered, servant-less two-bedroom apartment.

And while she browsed the titles, Sunil asked her to get comfortable and help herself to a drink of water if she needed some. Then he went swiftly to his room and bolted the door behind him. Monica hung around the bookshelf. After a beat, she strolled to the tiny balcony next to the drawing room.

Much to her surprise, there was another balcony adjacent to the one she was standing in.

Out in that balcony, a heavy-set mother stuffed a large fold of chapatti dipped in curdled dal into her three-year-old's mouth. 'Eat or else *bhoot* will come,' she warned, putting the fear of the devil in the little boy. Then, pointing to the street below, she said, 'If you don't eat, bhoot will come from there and take you from here and go far, far away.' Saying this, she stuffed her child's mouth with yet another bite.

'Bhoot' or the devil was supposed to come from the busy road below. Monica tilted her head down to see buses roar past. People were walking at a hurried pace. But a vegetable vendor who had her cart parked on the footpath below arrested Monica's attention. The lady was tall and buxom, wearing a large bindi. A man came and picked up a head of cabbage from her cart. Examining it, he asked for the price. She replied that it was twenty-five rupees. He bobbed the cabbage in his hand.

'Give it for fifteen,' he said.

The lady hastily took the head of cabbage back and stacked it in her cart. With a wave of her hand, she asked him to get lost.

'*Nahi dene ka hai, chal jaa, bhikari,*' she said and looked away.

Aghast at not only being denied the cabbage but also being called a beggar, the man muttered a curse and stomped away. The mother next door who was watching the drama said out loud, '*Array! Tch!* See, again you lost a customer.'

'I don't care. You go to hotel, you tell the waiter or what, give me bill for less? *Chup chap*, quietly you people give na? With GST?'

The little boy had finished his bite. 'Eat, eat, otherwise

Jana Bai will call bhoot.' Saying this, the mother quickly stuffed
another oversized bite of dal–chapatti into his mouth and
turned to banter with the vegetable vendor. '*Aga*, Jana Bai!'
she called out to the lady with rugged oomph to continue
their conversation.

Monica smiled at their theatrics. Sunil was bustling around
in his kitchen now. It was a large room, with an oversized
dining table. Sunil looked like a different person in his relaxed
capris and T-shirt as he placed a chopping board and knife
on the kitchen slab and looked around for something. Monica
walked up to him.

'I am surprised you read. I was of the opinion that
millennials did not.'

'Some of us do. Please, have a seat.'

At home now, Sunil was relaxed and that helped Monica
drop her guard as well. The mood was perfect for the stiff tot
of whiskey that he was now pouring for himself.

'Care for a drink? You may need one after the crazy day,'
he said. Monica was not sure as she had never heard of or
seen a bottle of Blenders Pride before.

'Ah, you must be used to single malts!' He was quick to
assess what was going on in her mind. Then, taking a swift sip,
he walked to the wooden cabinet. Opening the door, he pulled
out a medium-sized rattan bag with a thick rope attached to
it. Monica was taken aback when he went to the balcony,
called out for Jana Bai, and asked her about the vegetables
of the day. Next, he enquired about the cost. Taking a few
currency notes from his wallet, he put them in the rattan sling
and lowered it nimbly with the help of the rope. There was
a pocket of stillness after which he started to pull the rope
back up, this time with a thrust of effort. Next, he picked up

his bag, filled to the brim with pops of colour.

Back in the kitchen now, Sunil set out an onion, a tomato and coriander on the chopping board. 'Food will be ready in half an hour. You could use the other room if you like.' He said without looking at her.

'No, I am fine here. And I think I could use some whiskey as well.'

'Help yourself,' he said without turning to look at her. He was dicing the onions now. Monica poured whiskey into her tumbler and walked to the fridge.

'So, what's for dinner?' she asked as she opened the door.

'Khichdi,' replied Sunil without turning back.

'You like to cook?' Monica picked up a bottle of chilled water and shut the door.

'I like simple vegetarian freshly made food. And I eat frugally. Makes no sense to have a cook as my work hours are erratic.'

Monica added chilled water to the golden liquid.

'Vegetarian? Hmm… Sounds interesting. It will be a nice change for me. I was planning on going vegan for a bit, but never came around to doing it.' She took a quick sip. The whiskey–water blend was perfect. In fact, she quite liked the slightly raw taste of it. 'Cheers,' she said hoisting her glass.

Sunil smiled. He started to peel the skin off the garlic.

'It will be easy for you. You will just have to give up milk,' Monica elaborated further. Sunil said nothing. He was now crushing the garlic in a marble pounder.

'So, your family is in Pune and you are here. Does it get lonely?' asked Monica as she settled in her seat. Sunil looked up from his cooking and stared into her eyes.

'Only when I visit them.'

Monica let out a laugh. 'You are a loner?'

'I do like my own company, yes. No one to tell me what to do. It is nice to have a family but in another city.'

Monica started to snap her fingers. 'It is a statement by an author...'

'I know, but I can't recollect the name,' said Sunil.

'Speaking of authors, your love for crime thrillers is very evident.'

'And movies, yes.'

Monica looked back at the bookshelf. She pondered for a bit and taking a large sip said, 'But your collection is not just that of an avid reader...there is more to it... Do you dream of making movies someday?'

This time, Sunil stopped and looked up. Curious, he took a sip of his whiskey and asked, 'Why would you say that, Madam?'

'I just took a guess looking at all the stuff you have on cinema, sir.'

'Sunil,' he insisted that she call him by his name.

'Monica,' she replied pat.

Involuntarily, they both held up their glasses and chanted softly in unison, 'Cheers.'

'So, tell me about your love for the motion pictures, Sunil.'

Leaving his half-cut vegetables unattended, Sunil sat opposite Monica.

'It is funny. Actually, it all started because of my job. I had gone to do a security check for the MAMI Film Festival. Since my work was done, I thought to myself, "what the hell is a film festival anyway?" The first movie I watched was an old Spanish film called *All About My Mother* by this brilliant filmmaker called Pedro Almodóvar. And I was blown away.

By the storytelling, colours, music, and Penélope Cruz, of course. I was so taken aback that every day after duty I would go to the festival and see as many films as time permitted. I remember one day my shift was changed, so I would catch as many morning shows as possible instead. I was like a sponge, soaking in visuals, stories, colours, sounds, music...'

Monica nodded as she took a sip. 'Interesting. And then?'

Sunil cupped his palms around his glass. 'I started watching more films, reading books. This was about five years ago. Then after my stint with Altaf, I tried to—'

Monica sat up at the mention of Altaf.

'Sorry? What? What stint with Altaf?'

Sunil smiled and paused. 'Just relax. It's okay. He won't harm you. You are safe here.'

Monica took a deep breath and chugged a large volume of whiskey.

'Just a minute,' said Sunil.

Removing a cigarette from the drawer behind him, Sunil walked to the open gas ring and turned the knob. A blaze of blue flame burst forth. He tipped his cigarette gingerly into the flame and pressed the butt between his lips. Pulling a long drag, he made sure that the cigarette was inflamed.

'Actually, Altaf and I...we don't share the typical police–gangster equation.'

'O...kay...?' Monica drawled and leaned in.

'We got acquainted through another cop, he was Altaf's friend. Back then, Altaf was looking for a filmmaker to shoot his videos.'

'Videos?' asked Monica, placing her chin in the cup of her palms.

'Yes. You see, being a gangster is no longer a lucrative

career. That golden age of the Mumbai mafia is long gone. Altaf is now polishing his image as a do-gooder in his community. He wants to stand for the local municipal elections.'

Monica giggled, 'Really? He never mentioned his interest in politics.'

Sunil shrugged. 'I guess he was too smitten by you to tell you his future plans. Plus, he has not got his ticket yet. Could get embarrassing if he tells you and still does not have a ticket to contest the local elections, na?'

Monica squinted, trying to remember something. 'Yeah… actually the first time I met him he did mention he was a social worker. He insisted, not a gangster but a social worker.'

Both Monica and Sunil started to giggle.

'But later he would boast…"I shot him here, I sliced him there".'

'*Shining maar raha tha*, he was just showing off. His days are long gone. Now he is into petty stuff like *vasooli* and *mandavli*.'

'"Vasooli" is to extort money and "mandavli" is to douse the fire between conflicting parties. Right?' asked Monica tentatively.

'Superb! You have mastered gangster lingo.'

And both Monica and Sunil smiled like long-lost friends. Monica reached out for the Blenders Pride and refilled her glass. Sunil pushed his glass forward. As the golden liquid trickled down the tumbler, Monica said, 'Haan, so continue.'

'Basically, Altaf wanted a filmmaker. He tried to contact people. But no self-respecting filmmaker worth his salt would shoot for Altaf.'

'And how did you come into the equation?'

'Altaf happened to mention his inability to find a director

to my colleague, Inspector Dalvi. He knew about how I was teaching myself filmmaking from the Internet. Dalvi asked me if I would shoot for Altaf. I said I would give it a try. Altaf paid for every rental—lights, camera, sound-recording equipment, attendants, etc. And I had the time of my life learning with real equipment.'

'What did you shoot?'

'To begin with, vox pops.'

'What's that?'

'Short audiovisuals of locals. First, women and children saying how good Altaf is.'

Amused, Monica flashed a grin. Sunil continued.

'Then small-time businessmen saying how Altaf helped them. Then one day I shot images of a liquor store that Altaf shut down, starting a free library in its place.'

'This is crazy. I had no clue.'

'Maybe because he hasn't got the ticket as yet,' Sunil repeated.

'Hmm…'

'Anyway, I learnt a lot on that shoot. After that, I mustered the courage and shot my first short film!'

'Wow! So cool.'

'I have sent it to a few festivals right now. Let's see, *kya hota hai.*'

'You really are so passionate about movies. You should be a filmmaker. Why are you a cop?'

'Power. My job gives me power. And access. The kind that I will never have as a filmmaker.'

'So, you will waste the best years of your life compromising on what you love most?'

'On the contrary, I am making the best of both worlds.

Having a government job gives me power, access and security. It gives me the freedom to make my films.'

'But filmmaking is expensive. How do you manage that with your salary?' Monica stopped abruptly. Realizing it could be a sensitive spot, she tried to salvage the situation with an apology. 'I am sorry, I meant…'

'No, it's cool. Everyone knows cops don't earn much. Not on paper, at least.'

Monica smiled as she took a sip of her whiskey. 'Then how do you manage, inspector?'

Sunil opened his mouth but did not say anything. He looked around. Chopped vegetables lay unattended.

Monica realized it was an inappropriate conversation; too soon for him to be that honest with her. Moreover, booze, compounded with the adventures of the day, was clouding her mind like a fog. Monica now blinked her peepers gradually and drawled, 'Let's order, don't bother making anything now.'

'Ordering will still take half an hour. Are you good with Maggi noodles?'

Monica nodded and flashed a toothy grin. And then she passed out on the dining table.

13

*W*hile Monica slept in peacefully in a modest flat in Dadar, To-Be-Ex-Husband Raghu paced his cabin. He was trying to make sense of the mishap that had just taken place. A fleet of his vessels had mysteriously drowned in the Mediterranean Sea on a bright sunny morning!

And Abhay Suri lost his equilibrium when he found out that Monica was untouched in the truck accident and the truck driver was absconding! Moreover, time was ticking and the agencies were closing in. The family had to leave the country right away. There was no more time to waste now.

Back in Sunil's apartment, Monica's phone rang. However, she was in such deep sleep that even when she heard her phone ring, it seemed distant, as if it was for someone else. In the fog of her subconscious, she decided not to answer it. But her phone continued to ring with such dogged persistence that the only way to stop it was to turn the ringer off.

Now, tightly-shut peepers started to flutter gently as she reached for her phone. Monica's restful trance had disengaged her from the environment. Instead of silencing the annoying mobile, she involuntarily answered it. And when she heard the voice of her loyal attendant Manda on the other end of the line, she groggily ordered a glass of fresh orange juice, as was usual, at the beginning of any day.

Manda said that she would gladly bring juice but she needed to know where her Madam was.

Monica jolted out of her trance; her eyes opened wide as she looked around. She was in Sunil Bhonsale's flat, but worse, completely unaware of it.

On the other end, Manda sounded worried as Monica had been out since the previous day. Dawn, to be precise. Monica paused to think of an excuse. It was a lame one: that Monica was struck by such creative insight that she clicked pictures of churches from Bandra all the way north up to Marve. Moreover, she was on her way to Madh Island to click some more, she lied.

Manda was not convinced, but she knew better than to argue with Madam. Her Madam had been disappearing for long stretches of late.

Monica then ordered for some of her clothes to be packed. 'Keep it simple. Just jeans, T-shirts and pyjamas. Throw in a pair or two of my floaters…oh yes, and my make-up kit and creams, please.'

Manda complied.

'And, Manda, if anyone calls for me, just say you don't know where I am.'

'*Phone bajta kab hai ab*, Madam,' said Manda.

Monica realized she had a point. Who called on the landline anyway? If anyone had to contact her, they would call on her mobile.

Monica asked her to pack her stuff and wait for her next instructions. Then she hung up and hopped out of bed.

As Monica looked around, she realized that the flat was empty. The old grandfather wall clock began to dong. It was noon. Monica paused to calculate. She had slept hard for over twelve hours!

Monica went to the balcony. The sudden burst of sunlight pierced through her eyes and she squinted while looking around. With their clothes changed, the heavy-set mother, her three-year-old son and Jana Bai were minding their respective businesses.

In order to make her son eat, the mother put the fear of the devil in him while feeding him oversized spoonfuls of dahi–rice. Jana Bai was swearing at customers who were asking her to lower the prices of her fresh vegetables.

After the last customer stomped away, the mother asked Jana Bai how she could use such bad language while being a woman. *'Chee, aurat hoke kitni gandi gaali deti ho, Jana Bai!'*

'Moti!' said Jana-Bai to the mother, who did not seem to mind being called fat. The vegetable vendor then doled out a life lesson, *'Tu meri jagah khadi reh ke dikha. Do din main gaali dena seekhogi.'* Had she been in Jana Bai's shoes, she too would have learnt to use cuss words to safeguard herself.

The mother warmed up to the vendor and asked if Jana Bai had had a meal, *'Khana khaya?'*

'Main sirf tension khaati hoon,' Jana Bai replied that the tensions in her life were enough to keep her going. Monica smiled. Jana Bai then slanted a glance at Monica while the mother plunged another spoonful of dahi–rice into her son's mouth. 'Eat, eat, bhoot will come,' said the mother.

'Aye! Memsahib! You are saheb's relative?' asked Jana Bai.

Monica was taken aback by Jana Bai's effortlessness. Before she could answer, her phone rang yet again. Smiling tentatively at her two neighbours, she excused herself and took the call.

On the other end of the line, Manda was freaking out:

'Madam, someone has left big teddy bear outside our door.'

'A what?!'

'Teddy bear, Madam. Bear holding red heart.'

'What?'

'A heart. With "sorry" written on it.'

Worried, Monica put her hand on her mouth. She knew it was Altaf trying to make amends. Just then she heard her landline ring, perhaps for the first time since she had moved into her new flat. Manda shrieked.

'Phone has been ringing continuously, Madam. Not stopping only. But when I pick, no one talks.'

~

'You are getting blank calls. That is so 1900s,' said Sunil from the police station now.

'Listen, it's not funny. I am getting worried. Tell me, what do I do?'

'Nothing, just ignore.'

Monica shook her head in disagreement and waved her hand. 'Sunil yaar...I am getting worried. We have to make him stop.'

'The only way he will stop is if you don't react to him. Forget about him. And now I have a lot of work. So please don't call me.'

'How rude.'

'I am on duty.'

'Get lost!' Monica snapped. In the next instant, she realized that it was inappropriate to say that to a police officer. 'Shit—sorry, very sorry.'

'Hmm, okay,' said Sunil.

Just before he could hang up, Monica asked him, 'Sunil,

listen na. Last favour. I need clothes. Could you please send your constable Surekha to collect my stuff from my Manda?'

'Yeah, fine.' Sunil was getting impatient now.

'In plain clothes, haan…tell Surekha not to reveal anything, that she is a cop or anything.'

'Anything else, Madam?' asked Sunil coldly.

'What do you mean?'

'Can Mumbai Police be of any more service to Your Highness?'

'That's all for today,' said Monica playfully, blowing air on her manicured nails. Sunil hung up.

Gosh! He was so different last night, thought Monica. Just then, the doorbell rang. Persistently, without a pause.

Monica was on her guard now. Could it be Altaf? He had been obsessing over her and it would take him no time to find her whereabouts. Did Sunil squeal to him? Panic hit her hard like a punch in the gut. Monica was on the verge of tears. The doorbell continued to ring. Then, taking a deep breath, she gingerly peeped through the peephole. There was a frail old lady with hunched shoulders at the door. She wore a frayed cotton sleeveless nightgown and blue and white slippers.

Monica opened the door slightly. The old lady stared at her and asked, 'Who are you?'

'What do you need?' Monica asked.

'Sumi.'

'Sunil, you mean?'

'Sumi…that fatso… Array, the mad woman who makes her child eat saying bhoot–bhoot.'

'Oh! She is inside that door.'

'Gosh, I have become so forgetful.' Saying this, the old lady turned slowly and rang the doorbell of the adjacent flat.

Incessantly. Sumi came out and greeted her, 'What happened, *Aaji*?'

'My old man is not waking up. Just see if he is alive,' she said, irritated.

Sumi hopped across to the opposite flat. The old lady looked at Monica, worried. 'I don't want him to die.'

'Don't worry. I am sure he will be fine,' said Monica, consoling the stranger.

'Array, I meant I don't want him to die today. It's the India–Pakistan World Cup. Plus, my maid is on leave. Tomorrow she will come. Then it's okay.'

Sumi came back with a smile. 'Don't worry, Aaji. He is fine. Was in deep sleep.'

'Oh,' she said and went tottering into the flat. Sumi smiled at Monica, who smiled back at her. Sumi explained. 'Both sons are in the US. They live all alone.' Monica nodded and shut the door.

Relieved, she walked to the kitchen to soothe her nerves with a mug of warm coffee. While putting together the instant coffee powder, sugar and milk, the kitchen window came into view.

All her life, wherever she lived, Monica had rooms that overlooked different nooks of the Arabian Sea. Here in the housing colony, the view from any window was a matrix of other windows with routine life playing inside of them. Soon, she was closely surveying alien lives going in and out of the gates. Mothers escorting toddlers to playschool, an old lady with a large bag, probably going to the bazaar that was on the same footpath as the colony, a door-to-door fish vendor, household activities unfolding in boxes, a man smoking on his balcony, an older lady bobbing a newborn child in her arms...

She did not know the people or their names. Even their faces were not clear at that distance. And yet she was gazing. The simplicity of daily life was so fascinating that Monica realized she could stare out the window all day.

And then, on an impulse, she planted the coffee mug back on the table and walked across the flat. Pulling out her camera, she attached her oversized zoom lens and walked back to the window. Then she pulled in a sharp focus on the man who was now lighting his third cigarette. Through the viewfinder, Monica noticed he was striking furtive glances at the woman with the baby. She coyly looked his way and the baby gurgled a bit more. Monica started clicking the two at manic speed. She was in a flurry, actively capturing who she now realized were clandestine lovers.

Absorbed in her camerawork, she almost missed it when the doorbell rang again. This time it was Constable Surekha in plain clothes. Though she was taken aback at seeing Monica at the door, the policewoman did her best to hide her shock, and her stern face revealed nothing. Monica invited her into the flat for a cup of tea but Surekha mentioned she was on duty and left briskly. No wonder Sunil trusted her so much. The lady meant business.

Minutes later, Monica stepped into the shower. It was a simple utility bathroom with no frills. Monica looked around for a shower gel only to find a slim soap cake and the last dregs of an ayurvedic shampoo. Monica paused for a beat. She had never shared her bathing gels with anyone. She could not touch the soap cake. Making a mental note of sending for her toiletries soon, she had a shower using the ayurvedic shampoo as a body wash.

Monica spent the rest of the day clicking pictures of

unsuspecting members of the housing colony. By night she had submitted her assignment of fifteen images, fourteen from the housing colony and one of the steeples of Mount Mary Church that she had clicked the previous day, to Hormuzd Cawasji.

When Sunil Bhonsale came home in the evening, she poured him a glass of water. However, when she turned around to take the glass to him, she froze, rooted to the spot. Sunil removed a service revolver from the stiff holster attached to the left side of his belt. Next, a small pair of handcuffs followed out of a pouch attached to the right. Sunil then put both in the chest of drawers adjacent to the shoe rack by the door.

It was the first time Monica had seen a revolver in such proximity. Sure, she was aware that her father and husband both owned one or two, but it was something that was always tucked away in the farthest recesses of the cupboard as well as the mind.

Neither had they ever needed to use it, nor was there any reason for them to keep the revolver on their person. Sunil noticed Monica staring but did not say anything. He swiftly pulled out another pair of handcuffs from his pocket and, dumping them in, slammed the drawer shut.

Just then his phone rang. Sunil broadened his shoulders and stood ramrod straight. 'Yes, sir. Right, sir. I got a tip...no no, the four men, they are linked with the main man. Sir...'

Monica listened to Inspector Sunil Bhonsale with rapt attention. Everything he was saying was so alien to her. Words like 'lock-up', 'escaped from prison' and 'non-bailable' were unknown in her universe.

As he spoke, Sunil washed his hands. Then he went to

his room and bolted the door. Minutes later he walked out in a fresh set of pyjamas and a T-shirt. He was still having an intense conversation with Sir.

After a bit, Sunil was in the kitchen chopping brinjals with precision. Monica waited on him, and as soon as he hung up, she hoped to break the ice.

'What's for dinner?' she asked. Sunil was serious as he looked around for a saucepan. 'Preoccupied?'

'Hmm.'

Monica thought her presence was bothering him, so she went to the balcony. Sunil was not concerned with small talk or niceties that night. Half an hour later, when the meal was ready, he called her to eat. He had made a simple brinjal curry with steaming hot baby potatoes floating in it. And there was flaming red tomato rice.

'You are not drinking tonight?' she asked as she took a seat.

'No,' he said without looking at her, and sat down to eat.

'Why? Are you breastfeeding?' she said spontaneously and chuckled at her own joke. Sunil stared at her.

Monica was quick to apologize. 'I am sorry. I have this stupid habit of saying random things.'

Poker-faced, Sunil replied, 'I don't drink on Tuesdays and Thursdays.'

'Why?'

'Tuesdays for Ganapati and Thursdays for Sai Baba.'

'Oh…okay, okay.'

Sunil looked at his plate and started to gobble his meal. He seemed preoccupied. Monica gingerly spooned a tiny hillock of rice and bit into it.

'This is delicious. It is so simple and so satiating. You are a fantastic cook, Sunil.'

'Hmm,' he grunted and kept looking at his plate.

Tonight, Sunil was grim.

'Am I bothering you?'

Sunil finished the last of his food. 'No,' he said, and got up to rinse his plate at the sink. He was in deep thought.

Must be a moody guy, thought Monica as she slowly savoured her dinner. In the background, Sunil entered his bedroom and shut the door.

She heard him speak but the sounds were muffled. She looked out the kitchen window while she ate. The chain-smoker puffed away and the lady continued to be on the balcony.

Minutes later, Sunil came out for a drink of water. She looked at him. He looked back at her and shrugged. 'I am not used to living with anyone. So, if I am preoccupied, just let me be. Nothing personal.'

Monica nodded. He softened up a bit and explained, 'I am working on an important case.'

'Can I help?' Monica asked.

Sunil laughed out loud. 'So, what did you do all day?' he asked, changing the topic.

'I clicked pictures, mostly of the two of them.' She pointed to the clandestine lovers.

'Oh! The Smoking Bachelor and Mrs Radha Kerkar!'

'They seemed interesting.'

'They are.'

Sunil lit a cigarette, refreshed his drink of cold water, and through the film of smoke regaled her with a fascinating story.

Radha Kerkar lived in E-Block with her family. Her newborn son bore a striking resemblance to D-Block's Sandesh Pandit—the Smoking Bachelor, as he was popularly known.

To cut a long story short: ensconced in her mid-forties, Radha had three adult daughters. All her married life, poor Radha was cursed by her mother-in-law for not bearing a son.

Now dead, her mother-in-law must be very happy in hell because a boy was born to Radha. However, the resemblance to Sandesh, the Smoking Bachelor, was so striking that the only thing missing in the newborn boy was a nicotine stick between his tiny bunched fingers. And this was the entire colony's not-so-well-kept secret.

Monica listened to the story with rapt attention to detail. She was in the midst of so many lives, so many tales. There was the foul-tempered Jana Bai, Sumi the bhoot-mother, the geriatric woman who wanted her husband to die once her house-help was home, the Smoking Bachelor, and a policeman who shot propaganda videos for a gangster!

Monica raised her camera and froze Sunil's steely eyes in her frame. How she loved being here with him in that moment! She had so much to photograph here in this middle-class housing colony!

14

The next day, Monica woke up early. Rested and eager to seize the day, she would have gone for a morning walk with her camera, but for now she was safer under house arrest. *Self-inflicted house arrest, to be precise*, she thought.

Stepping out of the room she saw that Sunil was back from a morning jog. He was panting as he huddled to untie his laces.

'Good morning,' she said chirpily.

He motioned her to be quiet. That's when she noticed his smartphone glued to his ears. He sat on his haunches listening and then got up. 'I am trying my best, sir. But I am not able to trace the kingpin. Yes, sir. I will keep you updated.' Saying this, Sunil hung up. This time Monica knew better. She did not volunteer to help in the police investigation.

'You are really lucky you can go for a walk. Breathe fresh air.'

'You sound bright and chirpy yourself.'

'I guess it is the fantastic bedtime stories you tell me.'

Sunil smiled as he went to the kitchen to make himself some coffee.

'Would you not like a warm cup of coffee given to you? Frankly, I find it a nuisance preparing every meal.'

'But I quite enjoy it. Plus, I don't want to be dependent on anybody.'

Monica smiled and pulled out her camera. Trigger happy, she started to shoot the plain-clothes cop fixing himself a coffee.

'Why are you shooting me?'

'I have never seen an Indian man so independent.'

'That's by choice. I hate dependency of any kind.'

'Why is that?'

'Look, I like to live my life exactly the way I want to. I hate anyone telling me what to do.'

'Bad divorce?'

'Glad to be divorced! Marriage did not suit me. She wanted kids and loved all these family get-togethers.'

'What's wrong with family reunions?'

'They make such elaborate meals and fried food and force you to eat,' Sunil grimaced.

Monica smiled and clicked another picture.

Sunil continued, 'I'd rather spend my day reading books and watching films, or making them. I am most comfortable being alone, rather than with people. I don't think I can stay with anyone.'

At that moment, Monica's phone started to ring. It was Manda. Monica could hear the landline shrill persistently in the background. Manda complained that the phone had not stopped ringing. And just now, tons of floating balloons had been placed outside her door, all with 'sorry' etched on them.

'Madam, where are you? Please come home, I am getting worried.'

'Just do not open the door for anyone. Okay? I am fine and you will be fine too.' Saying this, Monica hung up.

Sunil looked at Monica. She told him about the balloons and how her phone had been ringing incessantly since yesterday, causing Manda to panic. Sunil calmed her down and promised her that he would handle the situation as soon as he got to the police station in a few hours.

'You have nothing to worry about. You are with me and safe,' he told Monica. She braced herself and walked to the balcony. Sunil went to his room. Half an hour later he was ready for work in his sharp uniform with his service revolver cocked in its holster.

He walked to Monica and assured her once again that he would sort out her problem right away. 'But Altaf cannot know of your whereabouts. And if I have to confront him, how would I know that there are gifts for you?' asked Sunil, thinking out loud.

'What if Manda lodges a complaint?'

'Not a bad idea. But let me work this through. Don't worry, okay?'

Instinctively, she put her hands on his arm and looked into his eyes. He blinked slowly and instilled faith in her. Monica stared at Sunil, and in that instant, she knew nothing could go wrong. With Sunil by her side, she was safe. And that's when Sunil left.

Monica's gaze lingered on the shut door. Touching him made her feel so safe…and warm. Sunil was someone she would have never met or spoken to, had life not taken a drastic turn. And none of the men she had met were like him. They did not cook for sure. There was something about the hands that packed a punch during the day and stewed wholesome vegetarian meals at night. His earthiness was sexy. No wonder she found him fascinating.

And all of a sudden, she wanted to be close to him. She went into his bedroom and lay on his bed. Touching the pillow, she drew his neatly folded blanket over herself and nestled in. She lay in bed for a long time, feeling warm, fuzzy and…wet.

Monica then stepped into the shower. And this time, she picked his well-used runny soap cake and glided it all over her body. This was the closest she could get to him. For he had made it very clear that he did not want the mess of relationships.

She thought about him. Sunil's simplicity was beguiling. Never, not once, did he make a pass at Monica. There was nothing sly or underhanded about him when it came to her. Despite the violence that his profession demanded, Monica found she was at peace around him, as well as in this house. There was no pressure. She could just be.

Oh my God! I am attracted to this man! Monica realized her folly when she stepped out of the shower. He was younger than her by a decade. She dismissed the thought… Maybe it was just the heat of the moment. Or maybe because she was trapped in his house, she felt attracted to the man who had rescued her from the bad guys. She couldn't be falling for Sunil. And she had not felt anything for him until now either. How could she have feelings after just one touch… No! It was wrong.

But then why did it feel so good?

Another phone call from Manda snapped her out of her reverie about the police officer. This time Manda was shrieking. '*Khoon! Khoon!*' she went on raving.

Monica panicked. 'What the hell happened? Manda, what happened? Talk to me.'

Manda informed her that a letter came in through the door and it was written in blood.

'What is written in the letter?'

'I can't read, Madam.'

'What do you mean you can't read? Just read the damn letter.'

'How can I read?'

'Manda, you are getting on my nerves now. I know you can read and write. Both Hindi and English.'

'But Madam, the letter is written in Urdu.'

'What?!'

'The blood-soaked letter is written in Urdu. All I know about Urdu is that it reads from right to left.'

Monica rolled her eyes as she thought for a beat. Next, she instructed her maid to collect the letter, balloons and teddy bear and go to Bandra Police Station. On hearing the words 'police station', Manda started to shake nervously.

'Sorry Madam, I am not getting involved in any police matters. Sorry.' Saying this, she hung up.

How dare Manda hang up on her Madam? Monica thought.

Monica redialled Manda's number, ready to give her a piece of her mind. For her part, Manda stared at the phone, and only after a few rings did she answer it. Monica took a deep breath and patiently said, 'Manda, I have a friend called Inspector Sunil Bhonsale in Bandra Police Station—'

Manda cut the call the minute she heard police station. Monica called yet again. This time she did not hide her irritation. She demanded Manda hear her out. But every time she mentioned 'police station', her loyal maid cut her call.

But Monica was just as adamant. She kept calling Manda, not realizing that Manda had decided she would not take her

Madam's call if it involved a police station.

This was very frustrating now. Her silly attendant was hanging up on her. She thought it was best to call Sunil. However, Sunil disconnected her call the moment it rang. Monica kept calling him and he continued to cut her calls.

He was at Mazagaon docks in search of two Kenyan cocaine dealers. But there was nothing he could find. All he saw was a small yacht that had set sail into the ocean. What he did not know then was that the yacht contained the four Suris, who finally managed to escape the country.

He hoped that the Kenyan suspects would lead him to his main target: the elusive drug lord called Cobra. His senior had been pressurizing him to nab Cobra, whose chain was responsible for distributing premium cocaine to the rich and famous in India. That was what was bothering Sunil for the past couple of days. He had to get hold of Cobra, but he had had no leads so far.

Now, he saw the two suspects, tall and well built. It was going to be challenging to overpower them. Just then, Monica called for the umpteenth time. Sunil switched his phone off and focused on the hunt.

When Monica figured out that Sunil had switched his phone off, she was livid. Seething, she started to send him text messages.

Sunil, you better answer my phone.
Sunil, I am in trouble.
Sunil, Altaf is sending letters and Manda is freaking out!
Sunil, Sunil…come on yaar.

Monica was getting desperate now. She tried to call Manda yet again. However, Manda did not answer her phone either.

Or respond to the umpteen desperate messages that Monica sent her.

Monica left Manda an audio message warning her. 'Manda, do not forget I am your boss. Just answer the phone. Hell hath no fury like a woman scorned, Manda!'

But Manda could not be bothered. She was busy collecting the letter, balloons and teddy bear and stashing them in one corner. There was something fishy. Monica was not home and was getting all these creepy presents. Now she was asking Manda to go to the police station. But Manda knew better than that. The rich messed up and the poor were the first to take the blame. She would have none of that.

Back home, Monica left audio texts in Sunil's inbox as well. 'Don't act smart with me okay... Just because I am living in your house does not mean...' Not knowing what to say to him, she cut it off there.

Monica had never felt so torn. On one hand, there was the fear of a gangster's obsession. And on the other, she was desperate to get Manda to listen to her. Moreover, she was clearly not important to Sunil, whom she had developed feelings for.

Monica started to panic. She walked to the balcony and drew in a deep breath, hoping the fresh air would clear her mind. It was two days since she had been cooped up in this apartment.

Just then, Jana Bai, the vegetable lady, called out to her. '*Shhoo shhoo! Shhoo shhoo!*' she called in the signature way people call out to each other in Mumbai. Monica looked at Jana Bai.

Then Jana Bai asked, '*Tu policewale ki badi didi hai na?*' Monica grit her teeth. She did not like being associated as

Sunil's sister. Elder sister, as Jana Bai put it precisely.

Jana Bai gleefully explained that at first, she and Sumi, who was feeding her child as usual on the adjacent balcony, both thought that Monica was Sunil's new girlfriend. However, Jana Bai insisted that since Monica looked older, she must be his elder sister. '*Ab Inspector Saheb thodi na kisi double umar ki aurat sey shaadi karega,*' Jana Bai grinned, exposing her paan-stained teeth.

'Just shut up, you bitch!' said Monica. Flaring her nostrils, she stomped inside. How dare Jana Bai call her middle-aged, a 'double umar ki aurat'?

For their part, Jana Bai, Sumi, and even her child stared at Monica, shell-shocked.

At that moment, Monica's phone rang. Manda was calling Monica to inform her that she was leaving her job. Monica sneered at Manda's empty threat. As her attendant, Manda had a cushy job with very little work. Manda managed the house, the cooking staff, the cleaner and chauffeur, and the easy needs of Monica. Neither was Monica bossy, nor did she ill-treat her. Manda had once said she had no one. Her parents were no more and she did not want to be a burden to her brother and his wife. And the handsome salary she got from Monica gave her respect in her village community where widows were thought of as ill omens, Manda had confessed to Monica. She knew Manda would never leave.

Monica let out a small laugh. A contemptuous one at that.

'How *can* you leave me, Manda?'

'Like this,' said Manda, and hung up on her Madam. She then retrieved her belongings and shut the door of the palatial flat.

Monica was stumped. She had just lost her loyal help of

over fifteen years. 'Oh my God. Manda has quit. Shit. Shit, shit. Shit!'

As Monica paced around chanting 'shit', there was a rap at the door. The rapping increased and she could hear women shouting out loud. Nervous, she looked through the peephole. It was Jana Bai, Sumi, and the frail, head-bobbing geriatric neighbour at the door.

Jana Bai insisted she open the door. Monica refused. However, Jana Bai persisted and kept screaming outside. How dare Monica call her a bitch?

'Bitch *kis ko boli?*'

'You called me middle-aged, double umar ki aurat!' said Monica from behind the door.

'But that you are!' proclaimed Jana Bai.

On hearing the insult, Monica grit her teeth and opened the door just enough to crane her neck out.

'Then you are a bitch too.'

The small group of women was enraged and pushed the door. But Monica was no weakling. She pushed with her entire weight on the door, making it difficult for the group of women to barge in. There was chaos and the old lady demanded that Monica apologize for calling her a bitch.

Jana Bai corrected the old lady and said she had called Jana Bai a bitch. The uproar got louder and they pushed at the door. As Monica was about to shut the door on the group, she saw Sunil come into view, and heaving a sigh, she let go. As a result, Jana Bai, Sumi and the old woman tumbled into the flat.

'What the hell is going on?' Sunil demanded.

'Saheb, your *didi* called me a bitch,' Jana Bai explained as she got up.

'My what?' asked Sunil with a frown.

'Your didi, *tai*, *akka*—whatever it is that you call your elder sister,' complained Jana Bai.

Sunil looked at Monica as tears welled up in her eyes. Sunil took charge of the situation. He apologized to Jana Bai on Monica's behalf and consoled the irate vegetable vendor, saying that Monica would be gone soon and they had no choice but to live together temporarily. A few honey-coated words here and there, and the policeman doused tempers and set the trio going.

He shut the door and looked at Monica. 'What are you up to?'

'Why haven't you been taking my calls?'

'Monica, I was on an important assignment.'

'I don't care. When I call, you answer, okay? Altaf is going crazy on me.' Monica started to howl.

'Look, I know that. But there is something sensitive I am working on. Yours is not the only case. It is not even a case—'

'Right. Mine is not a case. Everything else is important. My family wants nothing to do with me. No one has called asking where I am. A gangster is going batty with teddy bears, balloons and Urdu love letters written in blood. A police officer thinks that's not important. My maid has left me and that bitch Jana Bai says you won't marry me because I am a middle-aged, double umar ki aurat!'

Ouch! She did not mean to say the last bit! Sunil did not have to know that now.

A heartbroken Monica wailed out loud. Rushing to her bedroom, she flopped down on the bed. She cried into the pillow.

A moment later, Sunil entered the room and sat beside

her. Realizing he was next to her, she stopped crying and wiped her tears. She sat up.

Sunil spoke slowly, 'Age does not matter. But I will not marry any woman, whatever her age may be.'

Monica got on the defensive. 'Chill. I am not that desperate. Don't give yourself too much importance. Please stay within your limit—'

Monica stopped mid-sentence. She hadn't meant to say it. Sunil stared at her for a beat. Without a word he got up and left. Monica slapped her forehead.

In that instant, Monica felt the stab of unutterable loneliness plunge into her heart. Fear, anxiety and panic morphed into an abysmal low. This time, there were no tears. Just disgust.

~

Monica thought of Manda. Her Manda had always been there for her. And the poor help was scared. Was that wrong? After all, most people went to police stations, courts and hospitals only in dire situations, did they not now? Manda had always been at her beck and call; could Monica not accept her refusal to go to the police station?

And Jana Bai? The self-respecting vegetable vendor who Monica admired for her independence? Sure, she was coarse and her language was absolutely inappropriate, but could Monica not let it go? When did she become this crazy woman?

Where was her life going? Who was she? A woman dumped by her husband. Unwanted by her parents. She was taking refuge in a stranger's house because she was hiding from a gangster she had flirted with. She was now living with a policeman she would not have spoken to in the normal course of things. But she had fallen for him. And yet she had hurt him by saying things she did not mean!

Who was she? What was her place in life? Was she going to spend her entire life running from one man to another? Father to husband, husband to gangster, gangster to cop? Cop to...? When was the madness going to stop?

There was nothing for Monica to do at that moment. She could not go for a walk as she was under house arrest. She could not take a gulp of fresh air on the balcony as she had soured her relationship with Jana Bai. And she could not call Sunil.

Caged in, Monica started to scream into the pillow. Her violent muffled shrieks were followed by a burst of tears. Ashamed and lonely, Monica cried till she was completely spent.

Hours later, she fell into a deep sleep.

∼

When Monica stirred into semi-consciousness, she realized that day had turned to darkness. In her haziness, she saw Sunil throw a blanket over her. Monica huddled into its warmth and fell back to sleep.

There is no better cure than a long restful sleep. When Monica woke up the next day, she felt well. It was very early in the morning, almost 7.00 a.m. Monica calculated that she had slept at around 4.00 last afternoon, which meant she had packed in fifteen hours of slumber. It felt good. She woke up with renewed vigour.

She was so energized that she enthusiastically scrubbed her teeth and rinsed her mouth. She splashed water on her face, patted it dry, combed her hair and changed into a fresh set of pajamas and a T-shirt.

Sunil's bedroom door was shut. Monica decided to edit the pictures she had taken in Sunil's colony. Just as she opened her laptop, her phone rang. Looking at the display, she smiled. It was Hormuzd Cawasji. Her teacher was one person whose exacting standards had inspired Monica to make something out of her life. Taking pictures invigorated her and gave her a sense of purpose. The moment she took his call, he yelled, 'Congratulations!'

'Sir?'

'Your photograph won the second runner-up for Mumbai— The Era Gone By. It is going to be featured in *National Geographic!*'

Monica was numb. She couldn't believe that the two gorgeous middle-aged burkha-clad women hurling colourful swear words at one another in Altaf's neighbourhood would catapult her towards her calling. All she could ask Cawasji was, 'Sir! Really?'

'Not going to be on the cover page, so no paid internship— but hey, the good news is that every time they use your photograph, you will get a royalty of $150.'

'What?! Wow!'

'Yeah yeah, I know it's no big amount for you—'

'Sir, no. Please don't say that. This amount is priceless. This is the first time in my life I have made my own money. It was earned, not given. Something I created and was not handed. I have never felt this good...this free!'

'You should consider a career in photography. You will do well.'

'You think so? Will you give me a letter of recommendation, sir?'

'Um, I will think about it...'

The student and the teacher smiled simultaneously.

'Sir, please let me know if you hear of any internships as well!'

'Alright. In the meantime, keep practising. Bye.'

Saying this, Cawasji hung up. Monica felt like a brand-new person.

Taking a deep breath, she told herself that she was ready to face Sunil. Stepping out of her bedroom, she looked around. His door was still shut. However, this time she could hear indistinct conversation.

'Yes, sir... No, sir... I am trying my best, sir.'

When Sunil stepped out of his room, he was in uniform. He did not look at Monica and continued to put on his socks.

'Sir, all I know is that his name is Cobra. But I don't have a single trace of him. The way he looks or who he meets. Even the street peddlers have not met Cobra. Yes, sir, I have raided two rave parties. One in Pen and the other in Panvel, but Cobra has always given me the slip somehow.'

Sunil then nodded as he listened to his boss's spiel. Monica stared at Sunil. He did not look her way. Minutes later, Sunil opened the cabinet and cocked his revolver.

'Okay, sir. Have a good day.' Saying this, he opened the door to his flat. Monica put her hand on the door and shut it firmly. Sunil looked down, avoiding eye contact.

'I am sorry, Sunil. Very sorry. I was panicking yesterday. You know that I say idiotic things without meaning them. And yesterday I was getting cornered from all sides. Sunil... the thing is, I have feelings for you.'

Sunil looked up at Monica. She looked back into his eyes and continued, 'So when I was called "old" by Jana Bai, I was bruised. What I said was wrong. But I did not mean it.

It came out of not wanting to get hurt any further. I know it is futile to even think of anything between us. I am sorry.'

Sunil continued to look down, wordless. He twisted the knob but she shut it yet again. 'Okay, now listen to me very carefully. I am going to send you a number, trace it. It might just help you find Cobra.'

Sunil looked up at Monica and sniggered. That did not deter Monica.

'Trench. The party is called the Trench. Nunu—I mean, Manav Khanduja's exclusive party, held in the basement of his bungalow. Apart from premium cocaine and MDMA, young high-class escorts are available. They charge by the hour. Wives are not allowed.'

'If I am going to get my leads from rich divorcees on the run, God help me and my career.'

He opened the door and walked out. Monica looked at him. He turned around one more time and let out a snort before descending the stairs. Monica did not say anything and gently shut the door.

Next, she paced the room and looked for her phone. Minutes later, she sent Sunil a contact.

⁖

Sunil was walking towards his bike parked in the compound when his phone beeped. He checked his inbox.

It had the contact details of someone called Nunu.

What? Was this a joke? Sunil looked back at his window... Monica stood there waving. Sunil shook his head in disappointment. Straddling the bike, he kick-started it.

Monica turned around then, went to the kitchen cabinet and pulled out the rattan sling that had a rope attached to it. She went to the balcony. Jana Bai was setting up shop. Sumi the neighbour was feeding her son breakfast.

'Eat eat, else bhoot will come.' Sumi's eye caught a glimpse of Monica. 'See see, bhoot,' she said to her son, pointing at Monica. Despite being called the devil, this time Monica kept her cool and waved at the toddler who was staring at her.

Monica called out to Jana Bai. The woman glared at her.

'Sorry, Jana Bai. But come on yaar. Who likes being called "double umar" and all?' Jana Bai continued to stare at Monica. The latter continued, 'I agree I am an older woman, but you don't need to be so brutally honest, na?'

Monica looked at Sumi for support. Sumi had often told Jana Bai to tone down her harsh comments as it harmed business. Monica then leaned forward, put her palm on the side of her mouth, and informed Jana Bai that her 'M.C.' had started that morning.

This time Jana Bai nodded in solidarity. For every woman empathizes with another going through pre-menstrual mood swings.

'Sorry, Jana Bai,' said Monica yet again. This time Jana Bai smiled.

Next, Monica ordered a small amount of all the vegetables on display. She asked her for the value. Everything amounted roughly to ₹500. Monica put in two notes of five hundred and lowered the rattan sling. Jana Bai held up the two notes, wondering why she had paid double the amount. Monica explained, 'Double money from double umar ki aurat.'

Jana Bai smiled and started packing the vegetables. Monica turned to look at Sumi and smiled. All was well in this pocket of the universe.

∽

Tok, tok, tok. Sunil walked into the dingy, foul-smelling interrogation room. A handcuffed drug peddler squatted on the floor, shivering. A junior officer was questioning him while Surekha looked on. The officer's filthy abuses and slapping did not affect the steely lady constable.

On seeing Sunil, the suspect mumbled desperately. 'I don't know, saheb. I have never heard this name also. I have told you everything I know.' The drug peddler begged and looked into Sunil's deadpan eyes.

Sunil stared back. The peddler was an old hand in the trade. And Sunil's profession had taught him to filter what people said but also what they did not say in the process.

Sunil exhaled a puff of breath from his mouth and walked out of the room saying, 'Let him go. Surekha...' and then he asked his trusted constable to follow him.

Frustrated, he walked to his seat and slumped into his chair. Surekha came up to him. 'Sir?'

Sunil scrolled through his phone and reluctantly gave her a number. 'Track this number. I doubt you will find anything, but it is all I have.'

Surekha looked at the phone. 'Sir? Nunu?'

The assistant looked at her boss. Both burst out laughing.

⌒

Later that evening, Monica was opening up an oversized food delivery package when the call finally got through.

'Manda, I have been trying you since morning,' Monica spoke out loud into her mobile, which was on speaker mode.

In Dapoli, a village by the sea, Manda was drunk and not interested in what her Madam had to say. Her sister-in-law was frying plump bangdas, while her brother showered her with affection by pouring copious amounts of a transparent drink from a used beer bottle into her tall steel glass.

Monica asked her how she was doing, to which Manda grunted with a single 'Hmm'. Without wasting more time, Monica apologized right away and told her that Manda need not involve herself with the cops. That she, Monica, would sort everything out. Moreover, her job was intact. 'I cannot do without you, Manda,' confessed the large-hearted Monica. It is never easy to show one's vulnerability to a subordinate, after all.

Had it not been for the local alcohol, Manda would not have had the guts to drawl, 'Okay done, Madam, I come... *phor* you.'

On the other end of the line, Monica chuckled at her tone of voice and choice of words.

'Manda, you are drinking?'

'You Madam *log* drink grape wine, Manda drinks Mahua wine, flower wine. Natural, organic, farm to table.'

Monica let out a laugh. 'Get me some on your way back. We both shall have a drink.'

'Okay done, babe,' said Manda and finished her glass. Perching it on the floor, she signalled to her brother for more.

Tickled, Monica hung up. Lifting the plastic containers, she reached out for the tablespoons in the drawer.

৩

A quarter of an hour later, when Sunil walked into his flat, Monica was watching TV. She looked at him and said hello. But he ignored her as he stashed his gun and handcuffs away.

As he walked to the kitchen, he noticed a small dinner set out for him. There was a colourful stir fry of vegetables. He lifted the lid of the casserole and was greeted by a steaming,

Vrushali Samant

hearty sweet corn vegetable soup. Sunil picked a spoon and tasted the inviting soup. Then there was bread and an olive oil dip made with garlic, black pepper and cheery green coriander. On the side, there was a note. It had 'SORRY' sketched on it. Sunil picked the note and looked at Monica.

'Thought I'd give you a break from cooking,' she said. Sunil did not react. 'I am sorry, Sunil. I really am.'

It being a Thursday, Sunil washed his hands and sat to eat immediately. He did not invite Monica to the table. Instead, he helped himself generously to the soup. Monica went back to watching TV. Sunil poured the olive oil dip on the bread and ate heartily. The broccoli and peppers added some fabulous roughage, he noted. Making a mental note of adding salads to his otherwise grain-heavy dinners, Sunil ate his soup, bread and vegetables.

As he chomped on, Sunil noticed Monica staring at the TV. He dialled Surekha and deliberately put the phone on speaker so that Monica could hear:

'Good evening, did you get any leads from the number I shared with you this morning, Surekha?'

'No, saheb. All that I gathered was that this Nunu has a possessive wife. She has called him fifteen times, asking for his whereabouts. Feel terrible for him. But I don't think we are going to get anything out of Nunu.'

Sunil sniggered. Slanting a keen glance at Monica, he hung up.

This did not deter Monica though. She was mature enough to know Sunil was hurt and this was his way of getting back at her.

After finishing his meal, Sunil walked to the sofa and sat next to Monica. Jolted out of her trance, Monica looked at him and smiled. He did not smile back. Instead, he took the remote and changed the channel to a sports network.

The Wimbledon women's singles final was on. Barbora Krejcikova was raining fury on Jasmine Paolini.

'You know, as Wimbledon Debenture Holders, we used to watch so many matches up close and personal. We had premium seats and waiter service with luxury bars and restaurants because of our membership.'

Without reacting to this information on the lifestyle of the privileged, Sunil changed the channel. This time, Bollywood actor Anushka Sharma was cheering for the men in blue.

'You know, we were at Anushka and Virat's Mumbai reception—'

Before she could finish, he changed to a news channel. Donald Trump was on air.

'Trump Tower in New York—'

Sunil changed the channel, not letting her finish.

He stopped at a devotional channel. And then looked at Monica. This time, her forehead creased in a frown as a woman in a black robe chanted to an audience. The fair fifty-something woman with an unnaturally aquiline nose—an obvious cosmetic enhancement—arrested Monica's attention. Thick gold chandelier earrings hung from her ears, and she wore blood-red lipstick. Marigold petals decorated her shiny hair, which was slicked straight to perfection. The woman smiled beatifically as she chanted away.

'I am sure you have been to her as well,' said Sunil, voice dripping with sarcasm.

'Yes,' said Monica and slowly continued, 'did lots of her pujas and vrats and jaaps to have a child. She assured my husband that he would have three children. I was so happy!

How was I to guess that it wasn't meant to be with me?'

Sunil was at a loss for words. Monica excused herself. Sunil looked at her as she went to her room and shut the door.

Just then, his mobile trilled. It was Surekha. 'I think we have a lead. Nunu got a call from a man who asked *when* the Trench was.'

'Trench?' Sunil narrowed his eyes.

'It is a code word, I am presuming.'

'I am coming back, Surekha,' said Sunil. He hung up and collected his mobile, keys and service revolver. Moments later, he was out the door. Before shutting it, he looked in the direction of Monica's room.

⌒

As the hot shower water cascaded down her hair on to her body, Monica recalled snippets of conversations with Altaf.

'I am not a gangster. I am a social worker,' he had said during their first meeting.

'Altaf wants to be a corporator,' Sunil had informed her. He had shot videos for him.

Getting a ticket to contest the elections was the most important thing in Altaf's life, Monica concluded as she shut the tap firmly. Wearing her bathrobe, she wrapped her head in a thick Turkish bath towel.

Monica surfed online and purchased a rudimentary, outdated cell phone. Then she called Sunil. It was the wee hours of Friday morning and he had still not returned from the police station. When she called him, he answered immediately. Despite an overnight at the office, his tone was friendly.

Monica requested him for a new SIM card.

'Why?' he asked with genuine concern.

'I just need to start afresh. Too many memories on the old phone.'

'Okay,' said Sunil, and added, 'anything for you, Monica.'

15

$\mathcal{M}$onica was sipping coffee when Sunil walked into the flat at 8.00 a.m. He was carrying cans of beer. Monica noticed the spring in his step as he stashed two into the freezer while tossing a new SIM card in her direction.

'Thank you, Sunil. Truly, I appreciate it. You must be exhausted,' she said, holding her new card.

'What a long day, night and day! Very sleepy. Thought I'd have a beer and snooze for a bit. I have to be back by noon.' Sunil pulled out a chair.

'It is Friday, isn't it?' asked Monica, nimbly running her index finger along the rim of her mug.

'Yes. Why?' asked Sunil as he took a seat. He wanted to wait till the beer was cold.

'I have noticed that on Tuesdays and Thursdays, when you don't drink, you are very glum. And on days that you allow alcohol into your system, you are in a fantastic mood.'

Sunil stared at Monica, allowing her words to sink in. Her observation was bang on! Sunil laughed out loud. Monica followed suit. Getting up, Sunil pulled out a can of beer. Snapping the lid open he said, 'Cheers.'

Monica hoisted her mug and started mimicking Sunil on nights when he was not drinking. She made a dour face and chopped the surface of the table with her hand as if she was chopping vegetables. With a burr, she announced, 'I don't drink on Tuesdays and Thursdays. That puts me in a very bad mood but I hate to admit it.'

Endeared, Sunil looked on as Monica continued to imitate him. Surprisingly, he wanted this moment to linger. He quite liked cohabiting with Monica. She was so easy to live with.

ↄﾟ

Sunil was in deep sleep when the bell rang. Monica received the parcel of the mobile she had ordered. Then she flopped onto the bed and buckled down to insert the SIM into her new phone.

Once that was done, Monica walked hastily to the kitchen and looked out for Jana Bai's rattan sling. Stashing a wad of currency notes in the sling, she went to the balcony. This time there was no Sumi on the adjacent balcony. Monica was glad. Lowering the sling, she called out to Jana Bai.

Jana Bai looked inside to see a thick wad of notes. Then, cocking her head up, she asked, 'Are you and the inspector getting married? I don't have so many vegetables.'

'Think beyond vegetables, Jana Bai. I have some freelance work. Inspector leaves by 12.00. You shut shop from 1.00 to 4.00. Come over once you take a break,' ordered the memsahib.

ↄﾟ

Monica had no clue that she had a natural flair for acting as well as concocting lies. In Sunil Bhonsale's flat now, Jana Bai was reading a piece of paper. Monica had written lines on it that Jana Bai had to speak. When she looked up, Monica made a distressed face as she recounted her plight to Jana Bai.

And every time she repeated that she was a 'single woman', she noticed Jana Bai pushing her bangles up her arms and curling her fists involuntarily.

'There is a man who is harassing me, Jana Bai. Which is why I am here. I am a single lady just like you.' Jana Bai pushed up her bangles yet again. Monica continued, 'But I am not brave as you are. Please, Jana Bai, help me. I want to go back home.'

Clenching her fists, Jana Bai asked, 'But why is he harassing you? He is not your husband? Is he your *boy-pherend*?'

'I did not give you money to ask questions, Jana Bai. Just do the job. Please,' begged Monica. A fresh outpour of tears involuntarily burst forth, much to her surprise.

Jana Bai pushed up her bangles and nodded. Monica wiped her fake tears and dialled Altaf Sheikh's number on the spare phone. The moment it started ringing, Monica tapped her finger on the speaker.

'Haan hello? Altaf Sheikh?'

'*Farmaiyen.*' Hearing an unknown woman's voice on the other end, Altaf asked respectfully in Urdu for Jana Bai to state her command. But the vegetable vendor did not understand Urdu, which Altaf realized when she spat out a disrespectful '*Kya?*'

It was evident she had not understood what 'Farmaiyen' meant. So he asked her politely in Hindi what she wanted: '*Jee? Aap kya keh rahi thi?*'

Jana Bai squared her shoulders and thundered out that she was calling from the office of the political party, and that Altaf's ticket to contest the elections was getting cancelled. '*Haan main party office sey bol rahi hoon. Aap ka ticket cancel ho gaya hai.*'

The ground beneath his feet splayed wide open. Altaf lost his voice, and he was barely audible as he squeaked out the enquiry, '*Kyon?*'

Jana Bai loved that the sound of her voice had had a disastrous effect on a man. She stated emphatically that it was because he had attempted to kidnap a woman and later harass her by repeatedly sending her teddy bears and balloons.

Altaf denied the allegation vehemently, insisting that it was a *galatfaimi*. Yet again the Urdu word—misunderstanding, 'galatfaimi'—was lost on our Jana Bai. She heard it as *galat*-family.

Jana Bai thundered, '*Koi galat family nahi. Sahi family sey hain voh!*' No wrong family; the complainant was from a good family! Then, getting curious, Jana Bai asked what asinine adult male sent love letters soaked in blood. '*Aur ek baat bata, rey? Kaun bawlat khoon sey likhe khat bhejta hai?*'

Even more vehemently, Altaf denied that allegation as well. Why would he waste his precious Pathaani blood? '*Array, kyon kisi key liye main apna Pathaani khoon dey doon?*'

And after that he was back to his pleading self. He needed the election ticket at any cost. His future was at stake after all… '*Madam, please mujhe ticket dey do. Aagey sey aap ko koi complaint nahi ayegi. Mere career ka sawaal hai, Madam.*'

On hearing this, Monica heaved a sigh and directed Jana Bai to wind up the call. It seemed like Altaf had been sufficiently threatened to make sure he came nowhere near Monica again.

16

$\mathcal{L}$ater that night, Monica was in a deep sleep but the noise of somebody moving around woke her up. It was dark outside. Monica checked the time: 1.00 a.m. She got out of bed, and saw Sunil bustling about looking for his things. He had been gone all day. Dressed in a plain white long-sleeved shirt and jeans, he was strapping his watch standing next to the shoe rack. He then sat on the sofa and pulled up his socks.

'Hi. When did you come? And where are you off to?'

'Sorry. I can't tell you.'

'That's alright.'

'Police work is secretive.' Saying this, he got up and walked to a chest of drawers. Removing two Glock pistols and a Smith & Wesson revolver, he started loading bullets in each.

'Okay listen, I will leave tomorrow,' said Monica.

'Leave for?'

'Home, I am going back home.'

'No, don't. Not tomorrow. I will come back and then you go,' he stated.

Sunil put the guns in a duffel bag and pulled out two pairs of handcuffs.

'What are those for?' asked Monica.

'You don't know what handcuffs are for?'

Monica folded her hands and asked, 'Is that the only use of handcuffs you know?'

Sunil stared at Monica. In his work apparel now, he was a stern no-nonsense police officer.

'I do not know what you mean.'

'Surely you have heard of BDSM, officer,' Monica said keeping a poker face.

Sunil stared at her, his steely eyes revealing nothing.

'No,' he stated.

Maintaining her naïve tone, Monica went on to tell him how some people got sexual pleasure through tying hands, blindfolding, and even hitting.

'Have you ever tried BDSM, officer?'

'Madam, I do third-degree interrogation. If I slap someone, she will collapse on the floor.'

Monica paused for a beat, and then leaning in, she suggestively whispered that he could always go easy: '*Toh dheere se maaro na.*'

༄

Twenty-four hours later, Sunil slapped the girni patta on the table persistently. He stared hard at the handcuffed and blindfolded Cobra and Nunu, who were made to sit on their haunches in the stinking interrogation room.

Surekha was spouting incessant questions in the background and Sunil continued to slap the belt on the table. The effect was sinister. Nunu started to shake. 'I don't know anything, I don't know anything, sir.'

'Cobra' was stoic, unperturbed. He refused to say anything. All of a sudden, Sunil lost his patience and slapped the girni patta on Nunu's chubby cheek. Nunu let out a loud cry.

'Saheb. Saheb,' he pleaded.

'What?' barked Sunil.

Nunu pleaded for the police officer to go easy on the whacking. *'Dheere sey maaro na.'*

In that moment, Sunil thought of Monica. How she had teased him the previous night. And then, as hard as he tried, he could not bring himself to hit Nunu again.

⁀

Monica was packing when Sunil stormed into the house the next morning.

'Where are you going?' he asked. He was drawn to her.

Cobra had confessed under duress. And had it not been for Monica's lead, he would have slipped away. But Sunil did not mention anything about the arrest.

'Home. I had told you na,' she said, reaching out for her camera to stash it away.

He took the camera from her hand and blurted, 'Not now.' Next, he pulled her close to him and kissed her fervently.

Eleven minutes later, the three-year-old from the neighbouring flat was running frightened as the passionate groans of fornicating adults were alien to him.

'Aai, bhoot! Aai, bhoot,' he said and ran towards his mother Sumi, who was piling his plate with pulao for lunch.

That afternoon, the child gobbled his meal and asked for a second helping.

⁀

Monica's to-be-ex-husband Raghu was taken aback. And so was the stock market.

Out of nowhere, the share prices of his company had

started to fall. This despite a 150 per cent rise in revenues culled in by his Luckshmi.

Raghu had no plans of buying over a sick company; neither was there any scope for dispute, nor did he have plans to wind up the enterprise—the usual three reasons for fall in share prices despite skyrocketing profit. The shares of Raghu's company came crashing down faster than kilos on a keto diet. It just made no sense to him.

Raghu tried to think back on what could possibly have gone wrong. He started from the beginning. Whether it was his core team getting poached, or his valuable vessel sinking in the Mediterranean Sea on a sunny morning, these were mishaps that had no logical reason behind them. That's when he had an epiphany: the only possible explanation could be his break-up with Monica.

Over the past few months, Raghu had noticed as chinks had slowly and steadily crept into his business. And they had multiplied so fast that today his company was on the brink of collapse. Raghu had a strong intuition that his corporate misfortunes were due to the meltdown of his marriage with Monica.

It was a well-known fact that marriage brought luck. The luck of one spouse was shared by the other. After he married Monica, his business had flourished by leaps and bounds. The moment she disconnected herself from him, Raghu's fortunes began to decline. And Raghu was a great believer in luck. Anything that worked for his business worked for him. At that moment, nothing mattered to Raghu anymore but getting Monica back.

∽

Back in Sunil's room, Monica rested her head against his chest as he lit a post-coital cigarette. He felt invincible as he took the first drag of the day. He had made love to the gorgeous woman he was attracted to. Moreover, she had helped him nab one of the kingpins of narcotic trade in Southeast Asia.

'Cobra' could have easily escaped from Mumbai had Sunil not found out what the Trench was.

According to Sunil's lead, Cobra loved the sights and sounds of the Trench. The debauchery, sleaze and glamour were enticing for the suburban shanty boy who had plied his trade on the mean streets to become one of the most ruthless men in the cocaine business.

While he did not mention a word of it to Monica, on the other hand, she told him how she had safeguarded herself from Altaf. Sunil was impressed. After all, Altaf was desperate to contest the election. He would do everything to make that happen.

But it meant that Monica would leave his place now. And as hard as it was for him to admit, he quite enjoyed her presence in his home. He wanted her to stay.

'Wait for a day or two. We never know what Altaf might be thinking,' he said to her.

Just then, his phone rang.

Looking at the display, he swiftly answered it and went to the balcony so that Monica would not be able to hear.

On the other end of the line was Altaf Sheikh.

17

A few hours later, Sunil was in Altaf's cache to shoot videos. His henchmen Tahir and Ayan, whose wrist was wrapped in a bandage, were in the room as well. Unlike his usual gregarious self, Altaf sat forlorn while Tahir sang his praises: *Sheikh Saab helped a doctor set up a dispensary, got twenty-four-hour water supply to a police constable's chawl, and started a papad-making unit for the widows to become self-sufficient.* The idea was to make Altaf Sheikh look like a messiah to his people for the upcoming municipal elections.

Sunil nodded as he heard Tahir out and said, 'This Sunday, take me to all these places and I will shoot interviews of people in the chawl and the ladies of the papad factory. They will speak about how Sheikh Saab's efforts have impacted their lives.' Then, Sunil slanted a glance at Altaf. Shoulders stooped, he continued to stare at the floor. Altaf had always been well maintained and agile. But right now, his body was submerged in sorrow. He was looking old.

'Saab?' asked Tahir softly.

Altaf did not look up but grunted, 'Hmm?'

'*Ho gaya saab, aur kuch bolna hai?*' Tahir tentatively asked if there was anything else to say. Altaf shook his head no and dismissed the henchman with a wave of his hand. Tahir left.

Now it was Ayan's turn to praise Altaf.

But Altaf's mind was elsewhere. He stood up and walked to Sunil. Ayan was at a distance.

Altaf whispered, *'Bahut yaad aa rahi hain Monica ki.'* Sunil looked on at the love-sick Altaf who was missing Monica dearly. He said nothing.

Altaf then confessed, *'Mujhe ussey kidnap nahi karna chahiye tha. Darra diya bechari ko.'* After admitting that he should not have kidnapped her as that scared her away, Altaf pleaded softly, *'Pyar karta hoon ussey. Nikah karna chahta hoon.'*

Sunil Bhonsale did not know what to make of this forty-something Romeo who was proclaiming his love for Monica along with his noble intentions of marrying her.

'Kya kya nahi kiya maine?! Phool bheje, voh sorry wala teddy bear...yaha tak khoon sey likha khat bhi.'

In his hopelessness, he added, he had sent flowers and a soft teddy bear that had 'sorry' etched on it. He had also sent a letter written in blood.

'Yaar, aaj kal teenagers bhi yeh sab nahi karte Altaf.' Feigning concern, Sunil commented how even teenagers didn't write letters in blood these days. *'Kya zaroorat thi khud ko hurt karne ki?* Why did you want to hurt yourself?'

'Khoon mera nahi tha.' The blood was not his, said Altaf, and turned to look at Ayan's bandaged wrist. Sunil tried his best to hide the smirk.

'Main galat tha. Mujhe sirf sorry bolna hai ussey.' Admitting that he was wrong and all he wanted to do was apologize, Altaf looked up at the ceiling and wondered out loud where she could be. *'Ya Allah! Kahaan hongi voh?'*

Sunil did not respond and continued to stare at Altaf.

‿◦

When he reached home at 5.00 in the evening, Monica was pacing restlessly in his flat.

'Sunil, I am leaving.'

'Why now? Wait for a few days.'

'I can't. I need to step out and get some fresh air.'

'Don't be ridiculous! What if Altaf spots you?' said Sunil as he shut the door and walked to the kitchen for a drink of water.

'I am claustrophobic, Sunil...something's happening to me.'

'Take a few deep breaths and have some water.' Saying this, he poured chilled water into his glass and gave it to her.

Monica stomped her foot and snapped, 'Even when the terrorist Ajmal Kasab was in jail, they would let him out for a morning walk from 6.00 a.m. to 6.30 a.m. I read it in the papers!'

Sunil stared at her. She had a point. Fresh air and sunlight were the right of every living being.

༄

The sun hung low as it slunk seaward. The evening was brimming with life and colour. Children squealed and ran around, as they usually do, regardless of reason. Dogs trotted, keeping pace with the joggers; the peanut vendor announced his presence with a nasal twang; young heterosexual couples cuddled each other, and most people looked happy as their stress ebbed a bit on the sea-facing promenade that evening.

Along with his cronies, Altaf too had taken a break from their chaotic election prep to soak in the sun, sea and fresh breeze.

As Altaf revelled in the expanse of the promenade,

Sunil, on the bike, came into view. Altaf cocked a smile seeing a burkha-clad woman wearing a helmet seated behind him. He pointed in Sunil's direction and said to his cronies proudly, '*Array wah! Inspector ki girlfriend apni biradari ki!*' The Inspector's girlfriend was from their community!

As the bike gathered speed, sea breeze struck her nostrils and Monica's spirit soared. She was so invigorated that she lifted the helmet off her head to breathe a whiff of life. Just then, the veil flew off, exposing her beautiful face. Happy at heart, Monica planted a peck on Sunil's cheek. Smiling, Sunil accelerated the bike and sped out of the gangster's stupefied sight.

Monica was so thrilled that she could not keep her hands off Sunil. And that sent him in a tizzy. He took a shortcut back to his colony, where he hurried with the parking and walked as fast as he could into the building. Monica was a few steps ahead. In the enclosed stairway they lost their guard and started caressing each other as they climbed. Sunil was lost in Monica and her touch, and though he felt someone brush past, he couldn't care. Without bothering to open his eyes or apologize, he and Monica kissed all the way to the door. He fumbled for the keys as he continued to hungrily kiss her mouth. Then somehow, he managed to open the door and the two shunted inside.

Monica pushed Sunil a tad away from her, hastily stripped him down, and was on her knees.

Sunil was in throes of ecstasy when the door flung open. Altaf was at the threshold. *Shit*, Sunil realized that he had forgotten to latch the door in the heat of passion. Monica leapt like a deer and reached out for her shirt. She hastily wore her long T-shirt while Altaf simply stared at Sunil as he pulled his pants up.

Altaf asked very slowly, '*Maine do ghante pehle tumse poocha, na jaane kaha hongi voh?*' Not less than two hours ago he had asked Sunil where she was.

'You met him?!' squeaked Monica as she looked at Sunil.

The shirtless police officer was in the eye of the storm now.

'Police...police work...is secretive in nature,' he stammered. Turning to Altaf he said, 'And you did not ask me, okay. You asked Allah.' Then, impersonating Altaf, Sunil said, '"*Ya Allah! Kahaan hongi voh?!...*" Array, how can I come between a Mussalman and his Allah?'

Altaf was stumped for a beat. He then removed a gun from the small of his back and looked at Monica.

'*Dekh, tu free hai. Mujhe mera career banana hai.*' The former gangster assured Monica that he was not here to harm her as he had a promising career to focus on. '*Aur sorry. Mujhe maaf karna,*' Altaf's heartfelt apology for the hell he had put her through was not lost on Monica. And she knew she had nothing to fear from Altaf from here on when he gave her his word, 'Sheikh ki zubaan.'

Then, Altaf directed a glance at Sunil. The officer glared back.

Monica tiptoed out the hall and picked up her camera, house keys and mobile. While she started searching for something, Altaf clenched his fists and charged at Sunil.

Sunil stammered defiantly, 'I did not tell you because... because...like you in the past...I...I...I want to marry now.'

Monica stopped. Sunil went on and on declaring his love

for Monica. She leaned in to process the information…

Was he just saying it for the heck of it or did he really mean it? Had he fallen for her after all?

Forget him. What about her? Did she want to be with him at all?

There is no clear-cut, watertight explanation for human behaviour. A moment later, Monica tiptoed out the main door with her camera bag. Sunil frowned.

'Where are you going? I…I was going to…propose… marriage.'

Monica knew it was a lie. He was saying that to protect himself. And however great they were together, it was but a matter of time before the novelty of things would wear off. And marriage? Did she believe in it anymore?

Just then, Monica heard herself as she said out loud, '*Dobara vohi galati karungi, toh main bhi bokachoda hi banungi na?*' It was the same striking remark she had heard from Sunil Bhonsale in her car. 'If I repeat the mistake, I would indeed be a bokachoda, a dumb-fuck.'

Sunil stared at her. So did Altaf. And then, flashing a wry smile, Monica made a charming exit.

Altaf asked Sunil what she meant.

'That was a joke between the two of us,' Sunil shrugged.

Altaf aimed his revolver at Sunil's forehead.

'*Kya bol ke gayi voh!*' he roared, demanding to know what she said.

'The one who marries a second time is a dumb-fuck,' Sunil spouted instantly.

Altaf eased off his arm and looked away. He seemed dejected.

'W-what happened?' asked Sunil.

'*Maine toh teen teen shadiyan ki hain.* I am married three times over, yaar!'

The men stared at one another, and after a beat, they both burst out laughing.

18

When Monica rang the doorbell of her apartment, a sheepish Manda opened the door.

'Why are you looking so embarrassed, Manda? ...You have your boyfriend over?' she asked. Manda vehemently shook her head no.

When Monica stepped into the flat, she saw Raghu stand up from the sofa. He was waiting for her. Monica kept her camera bag on the dining table.

'I am sorry, Monica. I was wrong. I made a mistake,' said Raghu immediately. He then told her about the corporate mishaps that took place in her absence. About the share prices of his company falling, the ship sinking, and his core team getting poached by rivals... Monica heard him out patiently.

After he had finished his spiel, Monica asked, 'Luckshmi must have delivered by now, na?'

'Her name is Pallavi, yes.'

'Congratulations. Boy or girl?'

'Boy.'

'There you go. Finally got what you wanted, Raghu.'

'I want you, Monica. I realized my mistake. I want you.'

'And what about your children? Your wife.'

'Pallavi is not my wife. Not yet, I mean. We are still married, remember?'

'Oh yes, you are my soon-to-be-ex-husband!'

'I will make them very comfortable. You know I will. Let's get back together, Monica. Please.'

Monica stared at Raghu. And then she broke into a warm smile.

'Thank you, Raghu.'

Raghu heaved, 'I knew you would come back—'

'I always knew you to be selfish. And shameless too. Yet I would hanker for your approval. But no more. I am happy being by myself.'

Her phone rang. It was Hormuzd Cawasji. Before taking the call, she looked at Raghu.

'Have a good life, Raghu. You can leave.'

'How will you live alone?'

Monica smiled as she picked up her camera bag. Then, answering her professor's call, she walked to her bedroom and shut the door on Raghu.

Hormuzd Cawasji had called regarding an internship with the newspaper *Mumbai Day*. He warned Monica about the long hours and low pay, not least the back-breaking work. Was she up for it?

Her doorbell rang yet again. Moments later, a worried Manda entered the room. Officers from the Enforcement Directorate were asking for Monica.

Epilogue

'Thank you for your cooperation, Madam,' said the ED officer, shutting the file of the Suri embezzlement case.

Three months had passed, and Monica was sitting in the ED office.

She had been cooperative with the ED officers. Patiently answered their relentless questions, which lasted for long hours of the day. She came out clean during the interrogation. Since her family was absconding, she helped them seal the Suri assets.

Apart from Suri Charities at Haji Bunder, all Suri assets—Suri Manor, their fleet of cars, holiday homes in Panchgani and Goa, jewellery, bank accounts, offices—were seized. So were the superyachts, private jets and holiday homes bought from the bank money.

And Monica had done this without leaning on anyone else. But at the moment, she was getting late.

'Happy to help always. But now I will take your leave, sir. I am getting late for my shoot.' Saying this, she picked up her camera bag and walked out, her eyes sparkling, her conscience clean.

An hour later she was in the pit, jostling for space amongst mostly male photographers who were trying to secure the best possible angle to shoot the runway. It was the finale of the Lakmé Fashion Week.

Apart from the models, she was also asked to get images of the front-row guests: the A-listers. Bollywood stars, their spouses, actors, luxury atelier designers, prominent journalists, and most importantly the socialites.

A year ago, she would have been in the front row. Now she was in the pit. In that chaos there was a quiet moment of realization—that front row seat could not give her the freedom that the photographer's pit did.

Just then, the lights dimmed and there was a blackout. A spotlight, and then the first model stepped in. With her focus on the viewfinder of her camera, Monica was ready.

In that moment, Monica smiled. She was so grateful. For everything in her life. For photography, for the opportunity she had been given, for the men she had met and the experiences she had had. Grateful for the fact that she didn't have a child and was therefore dumped; grateful for being deceived by her family. Unintentionally, they had set her free. At forty, Monica was finally free to live. Just the way she wanted to.

Acknowledgements

Boman Irani, Anosh Irani, and students of Spiralbound. Thank you. *Madness in Mumbai* was written and rewritten many times over, through the course of the lectures.

Kapish Mehra, managing director, Rupa Publications. Thank you for your faith and it is great to team up once again. My editors, Gauri Chopra and Padma Pegu, are a dream to work with. Thank you, ladies.

Officers in service, Mumbai Police, who do not wish to be named. Your contribution to the novel has been immense. Thank you for combing through the drafts and offering insights and suggestions.

City historian Deepak Rao is a powerhouse of information. Your anecdotes on Mumbai were the inspiration for this novel. Thank you, sir.

Sneha Bawari Makharia, Seema Narvekar, Aliefya Vahanvaty, Farzana Sarup, Gayatri Singh and Sharmila Khan—thank you for your inputs.

Anika Telang, for making sure I worked on the manuscript every single day. Thank you.

www.ingramcontent.com/pod-product-compliance
Lightning Source LLC
Chambersburg PA
CBHW031959010726
47493CB00007B/2262